In Plain Sight

R.M. BRESLIN

Thank you so much for the support!

RmBreslin

ACKNOWLEDGMENTS

Mum and Dad
Thank you for always supporting and encouraging me in
everything I do and for being the most amazing role
models.

Ryan
Thank you for being the most incredible partner I could
have asked for. For always supporting my crazy ideas
and believing in me. For contributing to this book – and
my life – more than you will ever know.

Danny
Thank you for all of our writing nights. For helping me
and encouraging me through my doubts, but most
importantly…for all of the wine!

1

The smell of disinfectant stung Nicola's nostrils.

"Nicola? Nicola? The police are here to speak with you."

Her eyelids slowly drifted open again and she eventually focused on the two men standing at the foot of her bed.

One was tall – definitely over 6 feet – and quite slim with long limbs , but with a kind face. *Funny*, she thought. In a way, he reminded her of a Stick Insect.

The other was around Nicola's height and balding with a mean, cynical face. He introduced himself as Detective Braum.

Bracing herself, she cleared her throat.

'Stick Insect' flashed a full, white smile her way and walked closer, "Evening Miss Evans. We have a few questions for you, if that's ok?"

Nicola returned his smile and motioned to the chair at the side of the bed.

As 'Stick Insect' – or Jones, as he later called himself – sat down, he pulled a small black notebook from his pocket. Detective Braum stayed standing but, then again, he didn't strike Nicola as the relaxing 'I'll set you at ease' type.

"So, what do you remember?" Jones asked, leaning his elbow onto his knee for balance.

Nicola frowned, trying to string everything together, "Not much. It's all a bit hazy. Fragments floating back together now and again, you know?"

Jones nodded and smiled reassuringly, giving her the space to continue. She obliged, "I... uh. I remember he said something before he pulled me out from under the bed. That's about it, though. I remember the pain, and then it all goes dark."

Nicola moved her hand to the bandage on her cheek. The nurses hadn't allowed her to see it yet, but the size of the bandage told her all she needed to know.

Detective Braum shifted his weight, pulling her back to the present.

Jones continued, "Well, we can at least fill in some of the blanks for you. If you're up to it?" When she nodded, he moved closer, "Your neighbour, Mrs Polkin, called the station to report seeing a stranger around your parent's property on multiple occasions. We sent a car to investigate, but when they arrived, nothing looked out of the ordinary. Mrs Polkin called again a few days later to report loud noises; she said she thought they sounded like bangs and muffled screams."

Nicola itched as though a thousand tiny animals were crawling over her skin, but she said nothing as she nodded at Jones, willing him to continue. "Mrs Polkin told us that she had seen the man leaving the property and that his white t-shirt was stained with a dark substance. We sent another squad car to investigate, and when they arrived, they reported seeing blood on the door handle. They forced their way inside, and that's when they…" His brows furrowed as his expression grew grave, "…I'm sorry, Miss Evans, but they found your parents. Then upon further search of the property, they found you bound in the basement."

She looked down at her wrists, again seeing the bruises spread across her skin. She didn't need to look at her ankles to know bruises would be there too; they ached under the hospital sheet. There had to be more – *wait; what did he say?*

"Sorry, what was that? I think I'm losing my mind. It sounded like you said something happened to my parents." She almost giggled but stopped when she looked at the faces of the two men in front of her. Neither of them could meet her gaze, so she carried on, tears building in her eyes as she asked, "What happened?"

Jones took a deep breath, a sadness on his face, "We're still working on that. We'll know more once the forensic team has finished their investigation, but we were hoping that you could fill in some of the blanks for us."

She looked at him as he spoke but couldn't hear him. She couldn't hear anything.

In one fleeting moment, everything she loved had

been cruelly ripped away from her. She was never going to hear her mum buzzing around the house, humming and cleaning as she went. She was never again going to hear her dad's crazy stories from his past.

Nicola had never really understood the sentiment when people said they had a hole that couldn't be filled. Until now. Sure, she had bones and organs and skin, but she felt utterly empty. There was a bottomless, swirling pit where her stomach had been, and a giant chasm in place of her heart. *But I'm not ready*, she thought.

"Why didn't he kill me?" Her words tangled with her sobs. Jones and Braum looked at each other and then back at her.

Braum responded, "It could be anything. If you could remember something – anything – about him, that would help. Usually in a situation like this, the victims remember the attacker."

She furrowed her brows and stared at him, "I told you already. The only thing I remember is being pulled out from under the bed."

Braum raised his eyebrows before narrowing his eyes at her, "Strange… you were in a room with him for a while, but you don't remember his face…"

Nicola tried to sit up, not realising quite how sore she was until pain shot across her ribs, "Are you calling me a liar?"

"Not at all, Miss Evans. It's just… convenient—"

"Braum! Enough!" Jones barked. He shook his head and took over, "It could be anything, Miss Evans. It's not uncommon for attackers to keep their victims alive because they've formed an attachment to them. Either a parental connection or a romantic one."

Nicola scrunched her face through the tears, but then nodded in acknowledgment.

"I know it doesn't sound great but believe me, it's saved a lot of lives in the past. It could also be vital when the team creates a profile for him."

"He didn't…" She couldn't bring herself to say it, just motioned towards her lap, "…did he?" She couldn't handle the idea of that. The violation.

2

A warm, reassuring smile appeared on Jones' face again as he rested his hand on her shoulder, "The nurses did a full examination when you were brought in, and no, there's no indication or any sign of assault or trauma."

The relief washed over Nicola as if it was her first cool shower in a heatwave. *Thank you, God!* She thought, tears threatening to fall again. Trying to control her breathing, she spoke, "So, who did it? Do you have a suspect, or a line-up or something?"

The two men looked at each other and then at the floor.

Braum cleared his throat, "He was gone when the unit arrived at your house. We're searching the crime scene and surrounding grounds. Hopefully, we'll have enough samples to narrow the search soon."

Nicola's heart raced, her palms beginning to sweat. If they didn't know who he was, or where he was for that matter, how would she be safe?

Just at that moment, the nurse came in and directed her gaze at the two police officers standing to the left of Nicola's bed, "I'm sorry gentlemen, but it's time to leave. The patient needs some rest. I'll walk you out." Her smile was soft but firm.

Detective Braum clenched his jaw; his frustration beginning to show. Though when he turned and locked eyes with Rosemary, Nicola's nurse, Nicola couldn't help but notice his face soften and become almost warm.

Jones broke the sweet, wordless embrace by letting out a sigh, but covered it quickly with a tired smile, "Thanks for your time tonight, Miss Evans. Maybe we can talk again when you're feeling up to it?" She nodded and he stood, packing away his notebook, "Ok. We've posted two officers here at the hospital for your protection; they're right outside. Anyone that wants to get in here will be checked. We will find whoever did this. You just have to try and be patient."

Nicola took a deep breath and tried to smile genuinely.

Detective Braum cleared his throat, "Well, if you remember anything of use Miss Evans," He handed her his card, "Please get in touch."

Once she was alone, she shuffled around in the hospital bed, trying to get comfortable. She was frustrated with herself for not remembering more. Staring at the wall, pieces started flooding back. Fragments beginning to knit together.

The table at the foot of the stairs had given him away.

The bang woke Nicola out of a deep sleep. She sat upright in bed, listening out for more noise.

After hearing only silence and the sound of her own breathing, she settled back onto her pillow and closed her eyes, eager to return to the handsome stranger in her dream.

CREAK. Nicola shot up in bed this time, knowing that she definitely hadn't dreamt that.

She thought about calling out into the house; asking who was there. It had to be her mum or dad, right? Though something inside her told her that she was being too hopeful.

Sitting up as quietly as she could, she swung her legs around and placed her trembling feet on the floor. With her heart racing, she could feel heat radiating up her neck and onto her face. The kind of heat you feel when you experience real fear.

Nicola got to the door and, lightly gripping the handle, hoped that the creaking of the door wouldn't give her away.

Taking a deep breath, she flicked off her light, plunging the room into darkness and slowly pulled open the door.

She stared down the hall leading to the stairs, through a gap no bigger than a couple of centimeters, praying silently that she would see her mum or dad walk up the stairs and into their room.

When neither of them appeared, Nicola tried to reason with herself.

Her brain was telling her that one of them must have been downstairs, making all the noise. Her gut, on the other hand, was telling her that something was wrong.

Something felt very wrong.

"Come on, Nicola," she whispered to herself, taking

a deep breath and stepping out into the hallway.

She reached the top of the stairs and peered around the corner.

There was nothing there. There didn't appear to be anyone moving around.

Nicola smiled at her own stupidity. Twenty-four years old and still creeped out by the slightest noise. She was about to turn and head back to her bedroom when something came into view. Something that moved quickly.

There was a loud thud and the thing fell onto the stairs, a dark stain beginning to form in the glow of the lamp that had fallen. It wasn't a thing. It was a person.

It was her mum – and she wasn't alone.

Nicola was pulled away from the sudden, shocking memory by Rosemary returning to check on her.

She didn't know if she should tell her about her broken memories. *Are they real, or is it just my brain trying to come up with something to make me feel less like a failure?*

Trying to distance herself from her inner monologue again, she decided not to tell Rosemary just yet.

"How're you feeling now? Is anything coming back?"

Nicola frowned and shook her head, hoping to clear the fog beginning to build.

"It's ok," Rosemary continued, "It's only been 48 hours. I'm sure it will start to come back to you soon."

Nicola stared blankly at her wrists, "Like I said, only bits and pieces. I hope it starts to come back soon, though. I can't stand the thought of people looking at me the way that Detective did."

"Oh, don't you worry about him. He's been like that for a long time, you just have to know how to handle him. Lucky for you, I'm the best person for that job. I mean, I was married to him after all."

Rosemary appeared around the fifty mark, with thick, dark brown hair set on top of her head in a messy bun. She was a little overweight, but was just tall enough to carry it off well. Nicola had noticed she always seemed busy, yet she still made time for everyone.

Even though she was often rushed off her feet, she

always managed to say hi to the patients on her ward – including Nicola. They had hit it off and had bonded quite a bit since meeting.

Nicola couldn't hide her shock, "You were married to that Detective? What…why?"

Rosemary laughed as Nicola tried to backtrack, not meaning to cause offense. "We used to have a daughter; you know," Rosemary continued, "a beautiful little girl called Stephanie." Her voice trembled and broke as she lowered her eyes, "Actually, she would've been around your age now, maybe a little older."

"What do you mean would've been? What happened?" Nicola asked.

Rosemary's back stiffened at the question, apparently reliving something she had little desire to. She cleared her throat and absentmindedly smoothed her skirt, "Well, John…" She caught herself with a small laugh, "…Detective Braum. He was strict with her. He doted on her, of course, but was still very protective. I tried to get him to loosen the reigns a little, but that's just how he was. As is the case with most sheltered children, Stephanie eventually started to rebel. She was 15 years old when it happened. She'd gone to a party with her friends one night and just… didn't make it home."

"I'm so sorry. What happened?" Nicola whispered, torn between prying and needing to satiate her growing curiosity.

Rosemary took a moment, trying to find the right words to continue, "John didn't make many details known to the public, so not a lot of people understand why he is the way he is." She sat down next to Nicola's bed and couldn't stop fidgeting, "Stephanie had been talking to an older boy at the party and had ended up going out to his truck. Eventually the boy admitted to driving to a spot under Kennedy Bridge and trying to initiate some sort of sexual act. He said that Stephanie had refused, and that he had gotten so angry he just threw her out of his car and drove away, leaving her under the bridge alone in the middle of the night." Rosemary's breath caught in her throat; her eyes glazed. Sniffling, she continued, "According to him, the only thing that he was guilty of was overreacting in the heat of the moment. The next thing you know, Stephanie's body was found in a nearby landfill site…in pieces. We still don't really know what happened. After all this time, I guess John just… he lost a bit of himself when we lost Stephanie."

Nicola couldn't grasp what she was being told. She handed Rosemary a tissue from the box on the bedside table, "Here. I'm so sorry for prying. Are you ok?"

"Oh…yes. It just never gets any easier, you know? People will tell you that time is a great healer but really, you don't get over it. You just learn to live with the pain." She wiped her eyes and sniffled, "I just wish I'd been able to help him cope more."

Nicola lay back in the hospital bed, not wanting to push any further. Rosemary would open up if she wanted to. She stared at the ceiling.

Rosemary spoke again, startling her with the sudden noise, "It may be a good idea not to let on to John that you know about that. He's a very private person; especially about Stephanie." She jumped up out of her seat and seemed to snap herself out of the memory she'd been sucked into, "Now, let's get you tucked in – I'm sure you want some rest!" Rosemary forced a smile as she tucked the sheets in around Nicola.

They didn't talk any more. She worked in silence and then with just the slightest nod of her head, Rosemary was gone.

Thoughts of murder and betrayal whirled around Nicola's mind as she lay back and tried to drift off into, what she hoped would be, a sound and peaceful sleep.

Her stomach dropped when she saw another person slowly stalk over to her mother's body.

The person crouched next to her mother and nudged her, "You should've stayed in bed…"

She couldn't watch anymore. Nicola quickly turned and hurried back down the hallway, knocking into a side table as she went.

It must have been her adrenaline, but she didn't stop; not even when she heard footsteps coming up the stairs followed by a low chuckle.

She crept back from the bedroom door when he

appeared at the top of the stairs.

As she glanced around the room, Nicola became aware that she was severely deprived of hiding spaces. Silently cursing herself, she scurried under the bed, hoping that it wouldn't be too obvious.

Just seconds after she pulled herself under, the door slowly creaked open.

*She remembered all of the "do's and don'ts" from horror movies that she'd watched in the past. **Don't**; Breathe heavily, cry out or make any sudden noise. **Do**; Try to remain calm, keep an eye on the killer, and when trying to escape, never look back!*

He strutted into the small bedroom with such authority anyone would think he was taking part in a fashion show. "Come out, come out wherever you are."

There was dead silence before he continued, "I know you're in here."

Nicola watched as he approached her bed, trying to control the sobs beginning to escape her. Her t-shirt clung to her skin. Her fingers throbbed, betraying the grip she held on the carpet. She squeezed her eyes shut and pressed her face into the scratchy material, trying her best to stay still. Her ragged breath was all she could hear. Her heart pounded so loudly; she was sure he would be able to hear it. The bottom of her feet brushed against the wall. She couldn't retreat any further. Her tears began pooling against her skin as she held onto the hope that she would be saved before he found her.

All of a sudden, Nicola felt warmth pressed against her left cheek. A mixture of iron and...something altogether spicier filled Nicola's nostrils. The first was unmistakable; blood, but the second? The second was harder to place. Cinnamon, Nicola thought.

"There you are."

Nicola's eyes shot open.

She was covered in sweat, her chest laboured with a heavy pant. Automatically she put her hand to her cheek and felt the bandage that had been placed there.

Everything was real. None of it had been a dream.

She turned to the clock and hoped that the dull sound

of the ticking would help to calm her down.

She knew she wouldn't be able to sleep with the amount of light emanating from the overhead bulbs, but she was too afraid to be alone in the dark. Just beneath the clock, the door to the bathroom was closed. *I never closed that,* she thought, trying to piece together the events of the evening.

Maybe it was Rosemary? Or perhaps it was Detective Braum?

Her fear was telling her to press the panic button next to her bed – call for help – but her need to prove that she wasn't as weak as people thought overrode it.

She pulled back the covers and took a few deep breaths before placing her feet on the floor.

Trembling, she lightly placed her hand on the doorknob. All she could hear was her heartbeat pounding in her ears. Bah-boom. Bah-boom. Bah-boom.

"Miss Evans? Is everything ok?"

The voice startled Nicola; she hadn't even heard the door opening. The light from the hallway spilled into her room. She spun around and found herself looking at one of the most handsome men she had ever seen.

He was tall, over six foot, with dark brown hair and a gorgeously full beard; brown with the slightest hints of red, blonde and black.

His shoulders seemed to fill the doorframe, and his legs looked long and full – *made up completely of muscle*, she thought.

Her gaze shifted back to his face, and she had to catch herself. His eyes were the most beautiful shade of green-brown that she had ever seen, framed with lashes that made her slightly envious. *Oh crap – you're staring!*

She was brought back to the present by his gaze, "Sorry, what was that?"

"Is everything ok? I'm George," he said with a smile, "I'm one of the nurses that will be looking after you while you're here." His eyes narrowed, "As a matter of fact, what are you doing out of bed?"

Nicola thought about what she should say. She couldn't exactly say that she thought a mad axe-murderer was in her bathroom, waiting for her to fall asleep so he could come back and finish the job he started.

Clearing her throat, she decided to go with a simple, "Yeah, everything's fine! I thought I needed to go to the bathroom but... I... uh, I don't."

George smiled again, shaking his head, "Well let's get you back into bed then, shall we?"

George helped her back into bed, and the silence stretched between them as Nicola just stared. She couldn't seem to take her eyes off him.

He leant over her to reposition the cover and she took a deep breath of his scent into her lungs. *What a manly, strong scent* she thought, trying to place it.

"Warm cinnamon?" She said out loud.

George's head snapped down, and she scrunched her face, knowing she hadn't meant to verbalise the question, "What was that?"

Nicola blushed as she responded, looking anywhere but George's face, "I just...I couldn't help, but you were so close... you smell really nice..."

George looked at her with an amused expression and crossed his arms as he waited for her to elaborate.

She took a deep breath and continued, "Your aftershave has a hint of cinnamon to it."

Nicola closed her eyes, fully expecting him to laugh. When no such response came, she popped open one eye and raised her eyebrows; a wordless question.

"Wow, you have a very delicate nose! Yeah, I can't remember the name of it, it was a gift, but a lot of people have said that. Good nose!"

"Where do I recognise that smell from?"

Nicola was pulled away from the question by Rosemary entering the room, "Oh, there you are, George!" She smiled at both of them. Turning to Nicola, she beamed widely, "I see you've met George? I hope he's been taking care of you."

Nicola blushed, "He's been accommodating. He's quite efficient at tucking in." She looked at George, and they shared a smile.

Rosemary shook her head and smiled, "Ok, well if you kids need anything, you know where to find me."

"She's a mother hen, alright!" George said, sitting down in the chair next to Nicola's bed.

"Yeah, my mother's just as…" Nicola's smile faded and she dropped her gaze as reality set in once again, "I mean, my mother was just as bad."

George dropped his head, "I'm so sorry about what's happened to you and your family. No one should ever have to go through that."

Nicola looked at him, tears building in her eyes. She was trying to hold them back so that she didn't seem weak. She'd never liked crying in front of people.

"What you need is a distraction. If you're left alone in here with your thoughts, you'll go crazy. Believe me, I know!"

She blushed – what was he going to ask her?

"Do you read?"

"Excuse me?"

"Do you like to read? The hospital has quite a few books in the waiting room. I could bring you some if you'd like? I do that sometimes for our patients – it helps pass the time."

She felt like such an idiot. Although she'd have probably said no if he'd asked her out, a small part of her was disappointed that he didn't.

"Yeah, I… I love reading. That'd be nice."

He smiled as he stood back up, "Perfect! Well, once I've finished my rounds, I'll grab a few for you and bring them on over."

She watched him as he walked towards the door.

"I'm so confused," she whispered to herself as he disappeared out onto the ward.

This wasn't the time to be flirting with someone. Nicola knew that. She didn't even really trust anyone right now, but George's blazing stare had drawn her in and made her want to talk to him more; get to know him. It was quite a nice distraction from the emptiness, anger and confusion she felt. Her new reality.

R.M. BRESLIN

2

"He didn't have anything new to tell me this week.
I'm going out of my mind, Rosemary!"

Nicola's doctor had been to see her. She was hoping
that he would have more positive news for her… but nope!
He'd said that she had to stay for a few days longer because of
her *"injuries"*.

What injuries, she thought – her bruises had healed,
and she was feeling much better… apart from the fact that she
still hadn't seen underneath the pad on her cheek.

"Oh, come now, Nicola. I'm sure Dr Banford has a
very good reason for wanting you to stay here a little bit
longer. It isn't all bad, is it? You have some amazing company
even if I do say so myself…"

Nicola looked at her and, seeing the smug smile on
Rosemary's face, couldn't help but giggle, "I'm gonna go
insane in here, believe me…"

She trailed off as they reached the door to her room.
On the bed, as promised, were three books. *'Cell'*,
'Twilight' and *'The Girl on the Train'*.

"How interesting. I didn't realise you'd been to the
waiting room to get books. You should've said and I would've
grabbed them for you."

"I… uh, I haven't. I think they're from George, he
mentioned that he might pop by soon with some books for
me."

Rosemary laughed as she helped Nicola to the bed,
"M-hmm… well isn't that nice of him?"

She didn't pay attention to Rosemary's tone as she
left. It was obvious that Rosemary believed something was
going on with the two of them.

Nicola sat back onto her pillows and pulled open the
first book – *'Cell'* by Stephen King.

***

12

A few hours had gone by and Nicola was still reading. The book had sunken its teeth into her and wouldn't let go. The story was addictive from the first line. Stephen King was definitely a master of his craft.

"Did I do well then?"

She jumped, not having realised that George was there.

Smiling, she responded, "Oh, God! Yeah, this one's amazing. I mean, you lost a few cool points with *'Twilight'*, but I guess I can see past it."

He laughed with her and moved towards her, clipboard in hand.

"Time to check the machines again?" She asked.

"Yep, it's that time again."

He reached towards her so that he could turn the monitor to face him, and she flinched, "I'm sorry," she mumbled, "I keep doing that. Every noise… every man that goes past my door... ugh."

As she looked down at her hands, he spoke, "It's not going to be like that forever, though. Given what you've been through, it's completely normal that you feel that way. Give it time and you'll start to get back to normal, slowly."

Nicola looked up and smiled at him, hoping with everything she had inside of her that he was right. "So," she said, trying to change the subject, "Have you read any of these books yourself?"

"I've read *'Cell'* and… I will admit that I did try to read *'Twilight'* once…but I didn't get very far."

They laughed together and chatted some more until George's pager interrupted them.

"I'm sorry, I have to go… let me know how the book ends. It doesn't look like you're too far off."

She watched him as he walked away. Just before he disappeared out the door, she called, "Thanks again, I will."

He shot a smile over his shoulder and moved out into the traffic of the hallway.

What are you doing, Nicola? You don't even know him, she chastised herself as she dove back into the book in her hands.

3

It had been three weeks since Nicola had been discharged from the hospital. Three weeks since she'd been asked to identify the bodies of the two people she loved most.

She hadn't felt strong enough to go to the house after that and, perhaps more importantly, the police still didn't want her in there. Luckily, one of her oldest friends, Janey, had offered her use of her apartment as a temporary home.

She had always been a tad jealous of Janey. She was 24, the C.E.O of a large electronics company and a regular jet setter with an apartment overlooking the river.

Nicola, on the other hand, was 24, working as a secretary and living with her parents because she couldn't afford to move out on her own. She didn't know what would happen to her childhood home now that her parents were gone. How would she sort everything out without them? She didn't even know where to begin with organising their funerals.

The best things about staying at Janey's apartment were that the rent was already taken care of, there was food in the fridge, and she was never there, which was perfect for Nicola. She couldn't face the questions that came with permanent company – not yet anyway.

At first, Nicola was wary of every sound, but after a couple of days, she had grown used to the moans and groans of the apartment, and no longer feared the shadows.

Of course, seeing George helped to push back her fears.

They'd seen each other every few days since first meeting back in the hospital. He was a perfect gentleman and always let her take things at her own pace. He would bring her books and listen to her whenever she needed; he was just what she wanted. She did feel guilty for feeling even the slightest bit happy without her parents. For surviving.

She still didn't fully trust anyone, but George made her feel safe. Maybe she was a fool for trusting him, but she couldn't go on suspecting everyone of being a demon in the shadows; worrying that every face she saw was *him*.

She shook herself free of her feelings and tried to paint on a smile as she sat down next to George on the sofa.

"I'm sorry to bring it up," George said as his smile dropped. "But have the police gotten any further with their investigation?"

Nicola put her coffee on the table and sighed heavily, "Not really, which isn't making me feel very safe. I mean, there's a psychopath still out there. It has me looking over my shoulder, checking every corner." She stopped herself, squaring her shoulders before adding, "It just messes with me."

"Did you tell Detective Braum that you've started to remember things?"

"Yeah, we had a long conversation about it a couple of days ago. At first, I wasn't sure if I *was* remembering things, or if my mind was just making me think I was..." She trailed off as her gaze travelled to the window, settling on the sunset over the river. The simplicity of the way the colours of the sky reflected off the river drew her back to a simpler time in her memories.

She longed for normalcy; for the way that things used to be. Helping her mum with the cooking and having deep talks with her dad.

George's hand found hers and his eyes searched her face; she could tell that he was trying to find the words she desperately needed to hear.

That she was safe.

The truth was though, until the murderer was found, Nicola wouldn't be safe. She knew this, but it was easier to live in denial than to admit the truth to herself.

"Thank you for the past few weeks." Nicola said, staring at George's perfect face. All of a sudden, she remembered the wound forced onto her cheek by the monster that took away her family. She looked down at her hands, "You're quite the agony aunt, aren't you?"

George laughed and looked nervously at the coffee cup in his hands as he spoke, "Well I've had a lot of training in the past."

She giggled and he looked up, putting his hand under her chin. Her eyes finally met his and a surge of energy crackled between them. He leaned in towards her, but she slipped out of his grasp at the last minute; she couldn't help it. He'd glanced at her cheek and she was suddenly extremely self-conscious.

"I'm just going to freshen up. I won't be long."

She closed the bathroom door, shutting out the world.

What if he thought differently of her when he saw her bare cheek? When he saw the wound beginning to heal, which acted as a constant reminder of what she'd been through. At least physically. *It's now or never*, she thought to herself, trying to work up the nerve to pull the bandage from her cheek.

Slowly, she tugged at the corner of the white square, oblivious to what lay underneath. Rosemary had, of course, changed the patch, but she'd never once stolen a glance. She hadn't been allowed to.

Taking a deep breath, she opened her eyes to focus on the wound beginning to come into focus. It was messier than she'd anticipated, stretching across her entire cheek. It reminded her of the old zombie movies she used to watch when she was a little girl. No, surely not...*was that a bite?*

Her mind started swirling, that recognisable black haze working its way into her vision. *Oh no*, she thought, *I'm going to pas*— it was too late. She hit the floor with a thud, narrowly missing the sink as she fell.

Nicola came around slowly, groggily looking around the room. She didn't realise what had happened until she focused on George appearing before her; concern on his face. *My cheek!* She thought, frantically settling her hair across it, hoping he hadn't seen it.

"What happened?" he asked, reaching for her.

She held onto him, and he helped her up; encasing her in the safety of his muscular, yet soft, arms.

"I'm alright," she said, clutching tightly onto him, "I don't know what happened there. One minute I was up and the next..." She motioned to the floor.

"Let's get you out of here. Come and sit down on the couch." George gently steered her through the corridor and into the living room. Sitting her down, he asked, "Did you hurt your neck? You seem a bit stiff…" He put his hand to her neck, threatening to move her hair and expose her cheek. Nicola shot backwards in a panic but then forced a smile.

"Oh, no that's nothing. I think I just fell at a strange angle that's all. I'll be fine!"

In an attempt to put as much space between them as possible, she stood and moved towards the kitchen, shouting over her shoulder, "I'm going to get something a little stronger. Do you want anything?"

"What've you got?"

"Well, I'm having Moscato, but there's whisky and gin in the cupboard?"

He called to her over the back of the sofa, "Are you sure you should be having that?"

Nicola poked her head around the door; a look of defiance on her face.

"I'll take a whisky please."

A few minutes later, Nicola emerged with two glasses. She settled herself back onto the sofa and gulped her wine.

"So," she said, turning to face George, "tell me more about you."

He sipped his whisky before replying, "What do you want to know? I'm not that interesting."

They both laughed, and Nicola prompted, "I don't know… tell me about your family."

His smile faded, and he straightened his back, "Well, I suppose the best place to start is the beginning. I was put up for adoption when I was 6."

"Oh, I'm sorry," Nicola said, resting her hand lightly on George's knee.

He looked down at her hand, then back to her, "Oh no, don't be. I don't remember a lot from back then. I mean, I remember my mum telling me she loved me and that she was sorry. I remember her crying as she walked away from me and down the steps to the car. The last image I have of her is her sat in the back of the taxi, tears streaming down her face. Then she was gone. She just left."

Nicola noticed that he was tearing up, but instead of

drawing attention to it, she held his hand. It was her turn to find the comforting words except, she'd never been very good at that.

Seeing the heartbreak in his eyes as he relived the memory, Nicola felt closer to him. He'd been hurt and understood pain.

At that moment, he was the only person she wanted to be with. She felt as though she could be herself around him; no pretending that she was on the mend, no pretending that everything was getting easier. She didn't have to wear the mask.

Without thinking, she leaned over and kissed him on the cheek. He turned, meeting her gaze. What came next seemed natural; he moved her hair aside and leaned in closer, stroking her lip. The energy between them was electric and all-consuming.

Nicola broke away from the embrace, but George put his hand on her knee, softly keeping her in place. They sat like that for what seemed like an eternity before he spoke.

"You're beautiful, you know?"

She scoffed, moving her hair away from her cheek, "Even with this?"

"Even with what…?"

Their eyes met, and they shared a smile, inching closer together. When their lips finally touched, it was like a door had been unlocked in her mind. The pain had been so all-consuming that she'd forgotten how it felt to have someone. Ignoring her growing guilt, she curled her hand into his hair and pulled him closer.

Just for a moment, everything melted away, and she felt normal.

4

Nicola had spent an hour or so at the hospital, visiting the nurses. She'd baked Red Velvet cupcakes to say thank you for how well they'd looked after her, "I think I should probably get going now." She said, realizing that she had kept them from their work long enough.

Rosemary shot up. Nicola had never seen her move so fast, "At least let one of us drive you home?"

Nicola looked at her face, finding it all full of hope combined with just a hint of worry. She appreciated the gesture but refused to let fear rule her life, "Rosemary, it's fine. I'll go straight home, I promise."

The lovely nurse wasn't convinced but gave in, "Fine, but I want a phone call as soon as you get home."

Nicola rolled her eyes but realised that no matter how annoying the concern may have been, she was grateful to have another mother figure in her life.

Reluctantly she agreed, pulling her coat tightly around her.

Reaching the elevator, Nicola couldn't shake the feeling of being watched. It was silly really; the corridor was full of doctors and nurses, all buzzing around between patients.

Brushing off the feeling as paranoia she stepped into the elevator and the doors slid shut, sealing her inside. There were four floors between Nicola and the outside world. Usually, it was a long, painfully slow ride, but visiting hours were coming to a close and that meant fewer people to smile at and politely push past to reach the fresh, crisp air outside.

I spoke too soon, she thought as the elevator stopped on the second floor. She moved to the side so that there was enough room for whoever had decided that this would be their ride. The doors opened and she prepared a friendly, yet reserved, smile.

There was no one there. Just an empty corridor.

She held the doors open and peered down the corridor, in case the new occupant had grown impatient and was halfway between the stairs and the elevator. Her eyes fixed on the end of the hallway. More specifically, the shadow at the end of the corridor.

She couldn't be sure of it but thought that it looked eerily like the outline of a person. What made it worse was that they weren't moving. Just standing.

Staring.

The hairs on the back of her neck were the only signal she needed to slip back into the elevator and push the 'close' button. A little too hard for normal circumstances.

As the doors slowly began moving together, footsteps echoed in the corridor, growing louder by the second. Nicola's heart began to race. Silently, she started praying as she jabbed the 'close' button once more. Thankfully, just as the footsteps reached their peak, the doors shut, and she began moving again.

When the doors opened, she was on the ground floor. She breathed a sigh of relief as she stepped out of the small space that had been her protector, if only in her mind.

As she walked towards the main exit, the door to the stairwell opened, and a voice called to her, "Hey, excuse me? Miss! Lady in the purple coat?"

She turned, offering a smile to the doctor before her. She took a glance at his name tag as she responded, "Hi, yes… how can I help… Dr Jeffries?"

He was out of breath and trying to regain his composure, "I wanted to make sure you were ok." She looked at him, her face scrunched with confusion, but he carried on, "Well I was adding a few things to my new office upstairs – it's one of the first ones they've finished, you know?" There was no response from Nicola so he waved his hand in front of him in dismissal, "Anyhow, I was running for the elevator, and you closed the doors. I caught a glimpse of your face, and you looked positively terrified!"

She laughed nervously, "Oh… I'm so sorry! It was just a bit creepy up there, what with the lack of people. I'm sorry."

Someone approached Dr Jeffries and whispered to

him. Nicola didn't break eye contact with the doctor, still trying to apologise.

"Yes Ethan, I'm coming." He graciously accepted her apology and smiled as he walked away.

Strolling out into the cold night air, she kept her eyes up and her hands in her pockets, as she tried to slow her breathing. *That's too much excitement for one night!* To passers-by, she was just a cold and determined woman on her journey. What they didn't know was that she was scanning their expressions for signs of possible threat.

The crowd was full of unremarkable faces; an old lady here, a teenager there. No one struck Nicola as the murderer type but, then again, what did she know? Only what the movies and T.V. shows had shown her. *Yeah, reliable sources*, Nicola thought as she quietly chuckled to herself.

She reached into her pocket and had one hand firmly wrapped around a bottle of mace that she'd bought online. The other hand was tightly gripping her phone; three digits, ready to dial at a moment's notice. She'd hoped that she wouldn't need the mace. *It's better to be safe than sorry*, she'd repeated to herself as she'd clicked the purchase button.

Making her way through the crowd, she tried to be assertive, yet care-free, but the misunderstanding at the hospital had left her edgy. She couldn't shake the feeling that there was something wrong, but she couldn't figure out what that "something" was. Or if, indeed, she was imagining it, "Oh, calm down, you're just freaked out because of the elevator." She said to herself as she walked.

The ringing of the phone in her pocket made her jump. She pulled it out and looked at the screen, frowning; she didn't know the number.

"Hello?"

There was the clearing of a throat and then, "Miss Evans? Detective Braum."

She sighed and rolled her eyes, beginning to walk again, "Oh, hi, Detective."

"You sound out of breath, Miss Evans. Have I caught you at a bad time?"

"I, um... I... no. I'm fine. I had a bit of a meltdown in the hospital and thought I was being followed. It's probably just my imagination though." She let out a nervous laugh.

"Yes, I'm sure. I'm just calling to give you an update on the case. Can you come to the station? I have some things I want to talk to you about and maybe we can run through what you remember so far?"

Her ear twitched in response to a noise to the left of her, across the street. She looked over and, seeing nothing, responded, "Um, yeah sure. That's no problem. I'll be there in say, twenty minutes? I'll have to catch a cab."

"Miss Evans, where are you? I'll have a squad car pick you up."

Nicola relayed her location and then ended the call, settling in to wait for the squad car to arrive.

Standing alone in the street, she felt strangely exposed. There were only a few streetlights still working and therefore plenty of "dark spots" that she wouldn't have given a second thought to had it been the middle of the day. The fact that it was dark seemed to heighten every sense; every sound seemed louder and her gaze caught every movement – both real and imaginary. Her legs were like coiled springs, ready to run if she had to.

After what felt like an eternity, she saw headlights roll around the corner and held her breath; hoping that it was the squad car coming to save her from the darkness. She let out a long sigh as the red and blue lights appeared on top of the car. *Thank God*, she thought.

As the car approached, she noticed a tall, broad man walk out of an alleyway in front of her, one street over. When she saw him turn towards her and start walking, her stomach dropped. Of course, she had no way of knowing if he was a threat, but the hairs on the back of her neck stood on end, making her skin crawl. So much so, that she considered running to the car.

They were both approaching from the same direction. Chances were that if he wanted to, the man could be on her before the officer in the car could react.

With her imagination running wild, she silently willed the car to move faster.

When it finally pulled up she flung open the door, launching into the back seat faster than she'd intended, and almost spilling out the contents of her bag.

The man reached the car just as Nicola slammed the door. She stared up at him, sure that he shot a sideways glance into the car as he passed. Was that a smile? No, it couldn't have been. *I'm going crazy*, Nicola thought; despair creeping into her thoughts, threatening to pull her under.

The voice of the officer behind the wheel broke the hypnotic spell she was under, "Are you ok, Miss?"

She breathed deeply and smiled at him, "Oh, I'm fine. Just being haunted by the past, is all."

He looked back at her, unsure of how to respond. Instead of talking, he only nodded. She sank back into the seat, finally able to let her muscles relax.

5

"Take a seat in here, Miss Evans. Detective Braum will be with you in a minute."

The door closed abruptly behind her, almost as if she was an inconvenience to the officer.

"Thanks…" she mumbled, walking over to his desk. It was a mess; the very definition of chaos. There were files everywhere. Some were open, some were closed. Some even had crime scene photos spilling out of them. "How does he work like this? This is such a –" Nicola cut her muttering off. A file near the edge of the desk caught her attention.

A file called: *'List of Possibles – Evans'*.

She knew she shouldn't touch it. It was probably against the law for her to even consider reading it. Keeping her eye on the door, she reached her hand down for the file and bit her lip as she opened it.

It was exactly what she'd expected – a list of the people in her life. Apparently, Detective Braum suspected every single person she'd ever known.

Nicola scanned down the list and her eyes focused on one name: *George: previous charg*e.

"A charge of what?" She whispered to herself as she scanned through Detective Braum's scribbles, "Wait…what?"

She couldn't believe what she was seeing; *He was charged with rape*?

Detective Braum bulldozed through her thoughts as he thundered through the station. She panicked, trying to put the file back exactly where she'd found it.

She knew there was no way she'd make it to the chair before he opened the door, so she quickly moved across to the window, trying to keep her composure while she thought over what she'd read in that file.

The door swung open so hard that the blinds shook when it hit the wall behind.

"Ah, Miss Evans. Take a seat."

"Detective." She nodded in his direction, "So, do you have any new leads or any new ideas on a suspect?" She walked across to the chair next to the door, trying to hide the tension she felt.

Detective Braum was a puzzle to Nicola. He seemed completely disinterested in anything happening around him, but at the same time, he silently observed everything. He always seemed to be taking mental notes whenever he was in a room; never missing a detail.

Braum closed the door and circled her, "Before we get to that, I wonder, are you starting to remember anything else? Anything at all that might help us?"

Nicola furrowed her eyebrows, trying to piece things together, "Other than what I've already told you, I haven't remembered anything else. I'm sorry, Detective. I have been trying, I swear."

He shook his head as he sat behind his desk, "It's ok, Miss Evans. Don't worry, I'm sure we'll get *whoever* is responsible for this one way or the other."

The way he looked at her made Nicola uncomfortable. She immediately felt as though she needed to defend herself, "What are you saying, detective? If I could remember anything else, I would tell you. They were *my* parents, remember?"

The pair sat in silence for a time, Detective Braum never once looking away from her face. *Studying her,* Nicola guessed. Looking for any tell-tale signs of uncertainty or untruthfulness.

Seemingly satisfied with his inspection, Braum cleared his throat, "Anyway, we've done our routine checks on everyone in your life; Janey..." He reeled off a list of names, but Nicola failed to pay attention until Braum tapped his hand on the desk. Her eyes snapped up to meet his. Detective Braum moved around to the front of his desk and sat on the edge; his knee coming uncomfortably close to touching Nicola's as he spoke, "Well, the one thing I can say is that it's fairly routine to check up on people in the victim's life. The statistics speak for themselves; over 60% of violent crimes are committed by someone known to the victim. That's why we are looking into everyone you know, or have come into contact with recently, first." He cleared his throat again, clearly building up to the awkward subject, "So far, I've just found a few parking fines, driving offences and drunk and disorderly charges, for the most part. I understand that one of your nurses has been visiting you quite a bit since your release from hospital. George, is it?"

Nicola chose to humour him, "Yeah, we're... we're friends. Why do you ask?"

"How much do you know about him, Miss Evans?"

Nicola narrowed her eyes, immediately putting herself on the defensive, "What do you mean?"

Her bravado faded when Braum spoke, "I think you need to be careful around him."

Great.

"What makes you say that?"

He straightened his back, "Miss Evans, George spent the first few years of his life with his addict mother and her string of abusive lovers. When the pressure got too hot, she chose them over her son, abandoning him to the care system. He bounced around between a few homes, never staying anywhere for more than a few years—"

Nicola interrupted, shaking her head and rolling her eyes, "How do you know about that? From your background check?"

"Yes... but it was discussed when he was brought in the first time." She met him with a confused stare, so he continued, "Miss Evans, it turns out that five years ago, George was arrested and charged with rape."

That was it. She hadn't imagined it. It was all real.

Respond, Nicola, she screamed at herself internally, realising that Braum was staring at her and waiting for a reaction. She raised her eyebrows and laughed, trying to feign surprise. Mainly because she didn't want to believe it, "You're joking, right? George? That's insane."

The Detective's expression darkened, "I'm trying to warn you, Miss Evans. I think you need to be careful who you're associating with, at least until we find whoever broke into your home and killed your parents. I'm trying to do my job."

"It can't have been George. I only met him at the

hospital afterwards. God, it's concerning that I have to point out something so simple to a *Detective*."

Braum rolled his eyes and responded, "You realise that it was the first time you *met* him? It may not have been the first time that he actually *saw* you, right?"

She closed her eyes and stood, putting her bag on her shoulder. When he tried to press the matter, she slammed her hand onto his desk, speaking with as stern a tone as she could muster, "You must be mistaken. Just find the bastard that murdered my parents. If you do that, who knows? You might be able to protect me. Something you couldn't do for Stephanie."

The words left her mouth before she could stop them.

Anger flared across Braum's face and then something else. Regret? At that moment, Nicola knew that she'd crossed a line that would probably never be re-drawn, "I'm sorry, that was over the line. I didn't mean to say—"

Braum cut her off, "Don't be. It's the truth." He opened a file on his desk and refused to make eye contact, "I'll be in touch when I have anything new."

Nicola swallowed the disappointment she felt in herself. His mind had clearly gone back to a time he would've preferred to forget. "I...I'm sorry." She repositioned her bag again, looking at the ground, and walked out of the office.

She climbed into the back of the patrol car designated to take her home and dialed a familiar number.

"Hey, you. I know it's late but, do you mind if I come over? I've had the day from hell and could do with some wine."

George laughed before responding, "Sure, no problem. I'll have it ready for when you get here."

"You're an angel."

They shared a silent smile through the line; warm and affectionate.

Sitting back in the seat, Nicola thought about what had happened in Braum's office. She had a decision to make; she could speak to George about Braum's allegations when she saw him, or she could go with her gut and just believe that it wasn't true, "The second option, I think," she muttered, sighing, as she watched the city go by outside.

***

Staring at the stacks of papers on his desk, Braum couldn't ignore what Nicola had said about Stephanie. Mainly because, to him, she was right. He felt totally responsible for what had happened and hated himself because he wasn't able to find her killer.

Even though it had turned into a cold case, he still spent his evenings with a glass of whisky in one hand and Stephanie's case file in the other. He knew that nothing in the file had changed since the previous night, but he couldn't give up on it. Couldn't give up on her. There had to be something that he was missing, some key piece of evidence that could lead him to finally catching that low-life scum. Alas, there was nothing. No fingerprints, no blood, not even a single hair. That was the part that slowly ate away at him.

Braum wasn't afraid of a lot in life – he'd seen almost everything there was to see in his job – but he was afraid now. What if he couldn't figure this out in time? What if he couldn't stop whoever was doing all of this before they went after Nicola again?

He threw his pen onto the desk, furious with himself for letting it get so personal. She reminded him of Stephanie too much.

"How the hell am I going to do this?" He whispered to himself.

Jones knocked and poked his head through the door, "Do you have a minute?"

"Sure, come in."

Jones settled into the chair, "Everything ok in here?"

Braum scratched the back of his head, stretching out the muscles in his neck, "Not really. I feel like we have nothing on this case right now." He leaned back in his chair, "It's our job to keep people safe and we don't even know what the hell their intentions are."

"How long have you been staring at this case file?"

"What do you mean?"

Jones cocked his head to the side, "When was the last time you slept? You look like shit."

"Fuck you…" Braum rubbed the bridge of his nose and stretched, "Ah, you're probably right. I haven't slept in days. I just need a break on this case."

"Yeah, and we will but it won't happen if you're not one hundred percent."

Braum was silent. Going home and resting just seemed like failure to him. He needed to crack this case wide open so that it didn't end up going cold. Nicola needed that as much as he did…even more.

When he didn't respond, Jones added, "What's really going on? You've been slumped over this desk for the past hour."

Braum cleared his throat. He didn't want to have a makeshift therapy session right now, but he knew that it could be dangerous to keep Jones in the dark. If he kept everything bottled up, he would eventually explode and…well, that wouldn't work out well for anyone.

"Is this about Stephanie?" Jones watched him with a steady gaze.

"No, I just… I want to catch this bastard." Braum hit the desk in frustration, "I've been going over this file for days and I can't see anything. I'm missing something… it has to be in here."

"You aren't going to see anything new in there if you don't rest. You need to go home and sleep."

"I've tried. I can't sleep."

"If you don't go home and rest, you could get one of us killed out there. There is a whole team of us," Jones pointed over his shoulder, "who are working on this case *with* you. We don't just stop when you go home, you know."

If any other officer would've been so blunt with Braum, he probably would've had their badge. Lucky for Jones, Braum didn't mind his upfront nature. They'd been partners for years and sometimes Jones was the only one who could stop him being so stubborn.

"I suppose you're right." He gathered the loose papers together and handed them to Jones, "Here, this is everything I've put together recently. Call me if you find *anything*."

"I will, now sod off."

Braum nodded at him and checked his phone as he left the office.

He was made of tough stuff and just couldn't shake the feeling of failure as he got into his car. Not too long ago, he'd have been able to work with no sleep and still make a break in the case. "Ah, shit," he mumbled to himself as he pulled out from the parking lot and onto the main road, calculating how much whisky it would take to make him sleep.

***

Nicola arrived at George's apartment and was relieved when he opened the door to reveal a full glass of her favourite rosé wine, "Well, won't you come in?"

"Why, thank you, good Sir," She replied as she carefully took the glass from him, smiling. She'd put what Braum had told her to the back of her mind, refusing to believe it and let it ruin her only escape at that moment.

Several hours, and more than a few glasses, later, Nicola leaned her head on George's shoulder, "Wow, it got late." She yawned, glancing at the clock.

George stretched, "You know what they say? Time flies when you're having fun." Nicola reached for her bag, but he stopped her, "Why don't you just stay here? There's plenty of space in my room?"

"What about your roommate?"

"Oh, don't worry about him, you'll be sleeping with me." When she narrowed her eyes, he quickly tried to backtrack, "No, no, I mean... you'll be sleeping *in* there *with* me... or, you can sleep in there and I'll sleep out here or something…"

"That's refreshing. A guy that gets embarrassed, rather than tries to make a move. It's fine, I'm sure we're capable of staying in the same room overnight."

She started getting up but then stopped, "Oh wait! I don't have any pyjamas with me."

"That's fine… you can wear one of my tops. I'm a lot bigger than you, so it'll fit with no problem."

She returned his smile and held out her hand, "That'd

be a big help, thank you. Lead the way."

George took her hand and led her down a hallway, and into his room.

Before she knew it, she was curled up next to him and falling asleep.

***

A few hours later, George turned over and the movement woke her. Yawning, she decided to go to the kitchen for a drink.

She closed the door to George's bedroom as quietly as she could, trying not to wake his roommate as well as him. She cringed as she clicked the door into place, sure that it was louder than it seemed, and turned on the hallway light. When she turned, she jumped and clasped a hand to her mouth.

Stood in front of her was a tall, handsome man with a youthful face. He had a strong jawline and lips that women would kill for. His shoulders were quite broad and she noticed that he kind of resembled George in the looks department, but his face didn't seem as soft.

She was suddenly very aware of her lack of clothing; just a top and underwear wasn't exactly an outfit fit for socializing – even if all he could see was her legs!

"Oh, I'm sorry. You must be George's roommate. Ethan, is it?" She whispered, stepping away from the bedroom door slightly.

He didn't respond, he just stared; his mouth open with a confused and shocked expression on his face.
"You're...you...?" He managed to choke out.

"Erm." She tried to think of ways to break the awkwardness but couldn't, "I... well it's nice to meet you. Excuse me..."

She didn't feel comfortable squeezing between him and the wall, especially with how he was acting, so she just stood there, looking past him into the kitchen. After what felt like forever, he slowly moved to the side and let her pass.

The hairs on the back of her neck stood on end and her stomach felt a little uneasy. Something about him frightened her. Why did he just stare at her? Like he knew her or something…

One thing was for sure, she wanted to get back to the safety and comfort of George's room as quickly as possible.

6

Nicola couldn't wipe her showdown with Braum from her mind.

What she'd said to him made her feel sick. How could she have been so callous? She'd let her anger get the better of her and for the first time since meeting the Detective, she pitied him. Although when all was said and done, he was the last thing on her mind.

George had tried to call her but each time, she let it go to voicemail. Even after he'd been so kind to her the previous night, she'd woken up feeling conflicted about the situation. Her confidence in her feelings beginning to dwindle. She wanted to talk to George about it but needed time to think of the best way to approach it.

When her phone rang again, she looked down, relieved to see that the caller ID didn't read 'George' and instead showed Jones' number. She answered with a sigh, dreading what was about to happen.

"Hi, Miss Evans? This is Jones. I'm just calling to see if you are ready."

"Yeah, let me just grab my coat and I'll be right down."

Jones and Braum had decided that it would be a good idea for Nicola to go back to the house. They were hoping it would lift the haze in her memory and deliver them the face of the killer. After all, she had been with him for a while before the police found her.

With a heavy heart, she threw on her coat and closed the apartment door. As she descended the stairs, she tried to calm her nerves.

It was the first time she had gone back to the house since it happened. Would there be blood? Would the place be a mess? Would the binds that held her still be in the basement? She hoped not – hearing what had happened was one thing but seeing it? That was completely different. She didn't know what to expect, except that it was going to be a very long, very rough day.

George was supposed to go with her on her first trip back. To hold her hand, hug her and be there for her – all of the clichés – but she needed a little time to set things straight in her mind.

She got into the car and was greeted by a reassuring look from Jones, "You'll be fine, Miss Evans. I'll be right there, and any time you want to leave, you say the word. Ok?"

"Detective Braum won't be there, will he?"

Jones laughed, a smile spreading on his face, "Nope, you've dodged that bullet today. Just me."

She nodded and looked forward, on the one hand wanting to delay the journey for as long as possible but on the other, wanting it to be over quickly.

***

After a short drive, Jones pulled over and parked in front of the place that Nicola used to feel the safest. The place where she'd had her first sleepover. The place where her parents used to tuck her in at night.

To look at it now, you wouldn't believe that such a happy family used to live there. The garden was overrun with weeds and the house itself looked… cold.

Nicola and Jones stood at the front door; a simple slab of wood separating them from the darkness within. Taking a deep breath and squaring her shoulders she muttered, "I'm ready."

Jones nodded and moved forward, pulling down the police tape and pushing open the door. Immediately a wave of dread hit Nicola, but she ignored it and crossed the threshold.

The inside of the house was just as cold as the outside; both in temperature and in atmosphere. The air around Nicola seemed thick and full of sadness, although it didn't seem to bother Jones. *Maybe I'm just going insane*, she worried silently as he took her elbow.

Jones spoke, distracting her from her thoughts, "Shall we do a slow walk-through? See if that helps at all? Whenever you need a break or want to stop, just say." Nicola agreed and started walking.

The living room seemed fine; there was nothing out of place. All of the plants, vases and figurines were exactly where her mother had put them. It made her sad to see that the plants were beginning to wilt and die; truly a metaphor for the situation.

They carried on throughout the living room and into the dining room. Nothing to report there, either. They then made their way through the kitchen, and Jones put his hand on her arm, "Miss Evans, this is where our team found your father."

She stopped. Frozen in her tracks; she couldn't move. She couldn't even answer him.

To snap her out of the trance, Jones spoke again, "We found your mother over—"

"On the stairs." She croaked, speaking over him as she looked towards the stairs, sweat beading on her palms, "I remember…"

Nicola was thankful when Jones began speaking again, covering the cracks in her own voice, "We think that the perp broke in and started snooping around, making a lot of noise. Which, in my book, proves that the guy we're looking for isn't a professional. So that's something to go on, at least…" He put his hand on her shoulder before continuing, "Your father must have heard the noise and came down to investigate. There was a struggle, and the perp overpowered him. We think that that's when your mother came down to see what the commotion was. She saw your father on the floor and tried to run back up the stairs, presumably to you, but didn't make it. We think he caught her on the stairs and…well…"

She approached with trepidation, not wanting to get too close. Jones was a little way in front of her.

Just the sight of the stairs affected her. She couldn't contain herself anymore and collapsed to the floor, painful sobs flowing from her. Jones crouched next to her, not sure of how best to help but trying his best to console her with his words. She appreciated the care, though she wasn't really listening. She wished that George was there instead, his arms around her.

***

Eventually, Nicola calmed down and sat on the floor. She turned to Jones, "I'm sorry about that… it just didn't seem real. Then when I actually saw the places where you found them, I just… it all hit me at once."

He shook his head, "Don't apologise, Miss Evans. I'd be worried if you *weren't* upset. Do you feel ready to do some more?"

Nicola nodded and stood, holding the bannister as they ascended the staircase to the landing.

She motioned to the corner, "This is where I saw… I saw mum and… and someone else but I don't know who it was."

"M-hm."

Nicola pointed down the hallway, "That's my bedroom down there…"

Jones nodded as he scribbled in his notebook, taking down every detail. While he was doing so, Nicola made her way over to the hallway window on the landing, taking a deep breath and looking out at the street below. *It's so normal out there*, she thought.

She took one last scan of the road below and began to turn away, stopping when she noticed a man standing across the street. He was tall and very broad, but he was standing in the shadow of a tree so she couldn't really see much of his face. He was wearing a blue jacket and dark grey jeans, with a beanie on his head.

She couldn't explain why, maybe it was the paranoia, but the hairs on the back of her neck once again stood on end and she quickly turned to pull Jones over to the window, "Hey, I… I think that guy over there is watching us."

Jones looked around, even opening and leaning out of the window to get a better view, "I don't see anyone, Miss Evans. Are you sure it wasn't someone just passing by?"

She shook her head, trying to sort her thoughts, "No, I'm not an idiot. He was stood right there, staring back at me. He was wearing a black beanie hat, blue jacket and dark jeans… I think they were grey. Please, look!"

"I have, Miss Evans. There's no one there."

Nicola had another look out of the window. No one. The street was empty, save for a group of kids playing in one of the gardens. How could that be? He was right there…wasn't he?

Just as she began to question her sanity, Jones spoke up, "Look, maybe that's enough for today? This is quite a stressful thing to be doing, so it's no wonder your mind is playing tricks on you. We can go through the bedroom and the basement another time." When Nicola didn't respond he continued, "Come on, I'll take you back to your apartment."

Reluctantly, she agreed. There was no point in arguing; Jones hadn't seen him. He was there though. Just stood there, staring at her.

She found no comfort in Jones' presence; she only wanted George, but how? She didn't know where to begin.

***

Sometime later, Nicola breathed a sigh of relief as she watched Jones leave through the peephole. She'd asked him to walk her to her door, thankful when he'd obliged.

There was something about that man she'd seen; she couldn't get him out of her head. He could've been perfectly harmless – just a man taking shelter from the beaming sun underneath a tree – but for some reason, her gut just wouldn't let her believe that.

She turned on the tv and tried to shake the thoughts from her mind. Luckily for her, *'Ghost Adventures'* was showing, so that was her evening sorted.

Not too long later, the shrill ringing of the phone pulled her away from the screen. She cleared her throat as she picked up the receiver, "Yello?" There was no response, so she tried again, "Hello?"

Her stomach dropped as she heard heavy breathing and then a click as whoever it was hung up.

"Not another one," She breathed, "Maybe I should call Braum…" She hung up the receiver and tightened her arms around herself. At that moment there was a loud knock at the door, and Nicola grabbed her mace.

With nerves of steel, she reached for the handle and

pushed her face up to the peephole. Seeing who was on the other side made Nicola's heart race.

On the one hand, she'd longed to see George, but on the other, she couldn't get her chat with Braum out of her mind.

Taking a deep breath, she pulled open the door. His beard seemed darker; his face still as handsome as ever.

Her face must still have shown remnants of the fear created by the phone call because George immediately put his hand on her shoulder, "Are you ok? What's happened?"

Nicola's eyes started to fill as she shook her head, "It's probably nothing but I, uh…I keep getting these creepy phone calls, and it's starting to scare me now."

"What? Who from?"

"I don't know…there's never any talking. Just breathing."

George's brows furrowed, "How many times has this happened, Nicola?"

"This is the fourth one." He shook his head in response, but she added, "I think I'd better call Detective Braum so that he knows…maybe he can, you know, bug my phone or something? I don't know…"

George nodded, "That's probably the best idea right now. The police need all the help they can get. For now, though, I don't want you here alone. Either I'm staying here with you, or you're coming back to my apartment. I'm not about to take any risks with your safety."

Nicola's heart fluttered in her chest as she heard the words and she looked into George's eyes. God help her but her heart won out over the worries in her head, "I don't want to be here right now. Please, can you take me to the station? I think I should speak to Braum…see what he can do."

"Sure thing." George smiled, his stress pinching the skin around his eyes, as she grabbed her coat, her keys and lastly her phone.

***

"Please take a seat in here, Miss Evans."
She nodded in response and set her bag down at the

side of the chair. Lowering herself into it, she worried that Detective Braum would think she was lying. After all, he hadn't been the most accommodating and supportive person so far.

The door opened, "Miss Evans. I understand you wanted to speak with me?"

Clearing her throat Nicola spoke, "Um…yes. Detective, I've been getting some really weird phone calls lately." He raised his eyebrows at her, and she carried on, "Well when I pick up, no one speaks. There's just a lot of heavy breathing and then the line goes dead."

"Ok, so how many of these *weird* calls have you had?"

"I've had four so far."

His face seemed to harden, "So why didn't you come to us sooner with this?"

She sank further down in her seat as her stomach sank. She felt as though she was a child being scolded for doing something wrong, "Well I didn't think anything of it. I just thought it was someone trying to mess with me."

"Ok." He made his way around the desk and handed a form to her, "I'll need you to fill out this report form, and make sure to let us know if it happens again."

"Wait… that's all? You're not going to do anything about it?"

"I don't know what else you expect me to do, Miss Evans."

"Can't you put a tap on my phone or something? They're always doing that on T.V."

He rubbed the bridge of his nose, furrowing his brows, the stress of the situation obvious on his face, "Miss Evans, with all due respect, this isn't a television show. I don't work for the Special Victims Unit or any part of CSI. To tap your phone, we'll need a warrant, and the only way a Judge is going to sign one of those is if we can prove that we have probable cause that the tap will lead us to the killer of your parents." When she looked towards the floor, disappointment and humiliation radiating from her face, he spoke again, softer this time, "But if you fill in that form to the best of your memory and call me when it happens again, we might be able to put our request before a Judge. See what they think?"

"Ok… let's hope the Judge has enough common sense to see that I need you to monitor my calls."

"Exactly. In the meantime, we will canvas your neighbours and see if they've noticed anything – or anyone – out of the ordinary lately." He forced a tight smile and the silence drew out between them. She was about to speak when he waved his hand towards the door, "Do you need a ride home, Miss Evans?"

"Uh, no I'm fine. I have someone waiting for me outside." Nicola stood and straightened the bag on her shoulder. She moved towards Detective Braum's desk and reached out her hand, "Thank you, Detective."

Her disappointment had subsided slightly, but the humiliation was still quite strong. She had always been very easily embarrassed by the slightest thing. Luckily, Detective Braum had the good grace to ignore it, "Thank you for coming to me with this, Miss Evans."

7

"That's that then…" Nicola said with a sigh as she collapsed onto George's sofa. The level of comfort was indescribable. The cushions were so soft, and the fabric? It felt like she was sitting on a cloud.

George came in from the kitchen carrying two cups of hot chocolate. Handing her a cup and sitting down he asked, "So what's Detective Braum planning on doing about the calls? Is he going to put a tap on your phone?"

Nicola shrugged her shoulders as she took a sip, "No. He said that there isn't enough prob… prob… oh God, I can't remember what he called it. Something cause?"

"Probable cause?"

"That's it. He said that until he can prove probable cause, a Judge isn't likely to sign a warrant for a tap on my phones. I've filled out a report and have to call him if it happens again."

"Is that all?"

"Hey, at least he listened to me. I thought he'd look at me like I'm crazy and tell me I'm imagining it!"

George let out a strained laugh, looking over at the window. Nicola smiled as she glanced at him. She knew she was stupid for not bringing up the rape charge – Hell, her parents would've called her an idiot if they were there – but she truly didn't believe it. He never pushed her, never made her do anything and was completely respectful of her. Not only that, there was no mention of him actually being convicted in the file. There was just no way he did it.

"Thank you for letting me come over. I didn't feel like staying in the apartment tonight. I'm just so exhausted with everything."

George turned back to her, shaking his head and waving his hand, "Don't thank me, please. It's what any decent person would do. To tell you the truth, I was starting to get a little worried about you, what with you not answering or returning my calls."

Nicola's stomach lurched. Should she bring it up? Should she lie? Another battle between the head and the heart. She looked at him; confusion swirling in her head, "Yeah, about that…" She steadied her nerves, "Well, there's just a lot going on at the moment, and I'm still on edge. I'm just trying to figure out who to trust and how to cope, you know?"

He put his hand on hers, "You can trust me. I'm here for you."

She smiled in response. *Yeah until I bring up what's bothering me.*

He moved his hand up to her cheek and lightly stroked with his thumb. It seemed crazy to think that the last time they were in this situation, Nicola had been so preoccupied with the wound. She'd almost forgotten that she had it now. His touch ignited her skin and made her heart beat faster. They locked eyes, and she knew what was coming next.

George leaned in, but it was suddenly all too much; too much emotion, too many uncertainties.

She pulled away, still trying to maintain her composure, "I, uh…I'm just gonna use the bathroom if that's ok?"

He smiled and motioned over her shoulder, "Go ahead. You remember where it is, right?"

"Of course – back in a minute."

Well done, Nicola! Way to act cool! Preoccupied with her thoughts, Nicola didn't realise that she'd opened the wrong door. She was halfway into the room before she took notice that it was George's room and let out a little whisper, "Oops…"

She was about to leave and close the door when she noticed something she hadn't seen last time. A photograph on the desk. She knew she was in the wrong, but her curiosity took over. Picking up the photograph, Nicola found herself smiling. It was of a much younger George and another guy. They looked so much alike; same height, same build…if it hadn't been for their facial features, they could've been brothers.

Hmm…I know that face, she thought to herself.

She didn't want George to think that she was snooping through his things, so she returned the photograph to its home on the desk and moved for the door. She must've opened it a little too forcefully because she heard something drop. She closed the door and picked up the jacket that had fallen. A blue jacket. A familiar blue jacket. Then it hit her.

Her stomach churned as she stood up and looked at the row of hooks on the back of the door. Right in the middle of the selection of baseball caps was a black beanie. Now her stomach sank to her feet and her heart started pounding in her chest.

This was the outfit that whoever was watching her earlier wore. Identical. It had to be, right? It was too weird to be a coincidence.

What could she do? She was in his apartment; with him in between her and the exit. She had two options as far as she could see; go back to him and make up an excuse to leave, or stop being a victim and start taking control of her life. There was only one thing for it; she grabbed the jacket and the beanie.

She moved confidently to conceal the fear threatening to swallow her up, the fog in her mind making it difficult to think clearly. Making her way to the living room, she made sure to position herself away from George, the sofa filling the space between them.

"Hey, did you…" George turned to face her but his words trailed off into nothingness when saw her face.

Nicola stood behind the sofa with the blue jacket in one hand, the beanie clutched in the other, "Has anyone borrowed your clothes today?"

"What do you mean?"

"Has Ethan borrowed any of your clothes today?"

"Not that I know of…" he responded slowly, frowning. His face scrunched with a deep frown.

"Hmm…"

George smiled and shook his head, "I don't understand…"

"Well, it's just strange. When I did the walkthrough earlier, I was upstairs and I'm sure…I saw someone watching us from across the street."

He stiffened, "What? Why didn't you tell me this? Nicola, with the calls? That can't be a coincidence for –"

She cut him off, "No, I agree. It can't be a coincidence that the man watching me just happened to be wearing a jacket this exact same colour, and a beanie with this exact design." He started to get up from the sofa, but Nicola put her hand out, "Please don't get up." George frowned in confusion again and before she lost her nerve, she continued, "Why were you watching me?"

He shrugged, raising his hands, "I don't understand, Nicola. I swear I haven't been anywhere in those clothes today."

"Well someone has because these clothes were on a body on the other side of the street…*watching me!*"

He got up from the sofa and started moving towards her, "Nicola, I swear I have no idea what you're talking about. Why would I be watching you?"

She held up her hand, "Stop! I don't want you near me right now!" She knew she sounded crazy, but she didn't care.

He ran a hand through his hair in frustration and sighed, his face tense, "I've never even seen the house. You said you wanted me there for the walkthrough, but you never called me. I swear it wasn't me."

"This is so typical, it's just my luck. The one person I choose to trust turns out to be the one that I should run from!" Nicola threw the 'evidence' at George, "Although, it shouldn't surprise me after what I found out about you the other day. I can't believe I was so cruel to Braum when he was right to warn me."

"Warn you? Warn you about what? I haven't done anything! Nicola, you're sounding crazy right now." George looked at her, pleading with his eyes and inching closer to her.

"Oh, so I'm crazy now? Wow. Thanks for that Mr. Rapist." George stopped moving, his hands now resting at his sides, "Braum told me about you."

"Mr what? He told you what? Please, Nicola, I don't understand."

"The rape charge, George! That's what I'm talking about. You've got a history of being dangerous around women and I was stupid enough to believe it wasn't true!"

His face dropped, and Nicola's heart sank.

"Nicola, I can explain all that. It's not what you think! I never touched anyone."

She let out a disbelieving laugh and said, "So was it you that broke into the house that night? What were you wanting to take? Surely it can't have been the plan to kill my parents so what… did they surprise you?" Her voice trailed off. It was as if it had been sucked right out of her. She just stood there, trying to breathe slowly and calm herself down.

"Nicola, please. Listen to me."

She turned her head and clamped her eyes shut, an icy wall of defiance radiated off her, "I don't want to hear it. I'm leaving and I'm telling Braum all about you."

She opened the door slammed into what felt like a wall. Gasping, she looked up and saw Ethan.

"Oh, hi…" His size at that moment was intimidating; sweat began beading on her palms and her chest tightened.

"I'm sorry…" She interrupted and slipped past, fully aware that George was hot on her heels, pleading for her to listen to him. She couldn't. She couldn't let herself be drawn back in. Maybe he didn't kill her parents, maybe he did. All she knew, as she thundered down the stairs and out onto the street, was that she was tired of being a victim and needed to do whatever she had to to keep herself safe.

She could still hear George behind her. He'd followed her onto the street and was trying to make her turn and give him a chance. He hooked his hand around her arm, spinning her towards him, but didn't expect the palm that smacked against the side of his face, "Don't touch me." Her voice broke, but her words were full of purpose.

She backed away from him and hailed the taxi approaching from down the street. Slipping into the back seat, she pulled out her phone and gave the address of the police station.

Against her better judgement, she turned to look at George as the car pulled away from the kerb. His face was haunting; full of loss and regret, but no anger.

"Hi, Detective Braum?"

"Miss Evans? Are you ok?"

She sniffed tears back and replied, "I'm on my way to the station. I've got something you might want to know."

8

"Miss Evans, please take a seat. What happened?" Detective Braum settled onto the corner of the desk, while Nicola sat down on the plastic chair.

Taking a deep breath, she responded, "I…I don't know if Jones told you, but when we were at the house, I thought I saw a man outside watching me through the window. Jones didn't see him, of course, but I'm so sure he was there. He was tall and quite broad, wearing a blue jacket and a beanie. I didn't think anything of it at the time, but something happened today and I… I wanted to apologise to you."

Detective Braum looked at her and nodded.

She continued, "After the walkthrough, I went to George's apartment. I didn't believe you and I just… I just needed to relax and… I don't know but I just wanted to believe that he was good!" She sniffled and wiped a tear before speaking again, "I wasn't snooping; I didn't even realise that the man outside my house had the same build as George! Tall, broad…anyway, I found…I found them!"

Detective Braum frowned. "I don't quite follow."

"I found the jacket and the hat. It's not like the jacket was black and the beanie was blank; the jacket was a funky blue and the beanie had a design on it. I mean, isn't it odd? Put two and two together and you come up with George. Why would he be watching me at my house? Was he looking out for me and making sure I was safe or…?" She paused and swallowed loudly, "…or was he there to revel in my sadness… going back to the scene of his crime?"

Braum waved his hand at her as if to snap her out of a trance, "But… Miss Evans. A lot of people have jackets and beanies."

Nicola stared in disbelief, "I know, and I know I sound crazy but come on? It can't be a coincidence. How many people have the jacket and beanie *plus* the size and build to go with it?"

Braum frowned, "All I'm saying is that there isn't a

lot to go on here. But we will bring him in for questioning. You never know, he might have something that will help us. If it *was* him outside your house, he may have seen something that will help crack the case."

She relaxed, sinking into her chair, "Thank you. I just… I can't believe it. He didn't even try to deny it when I confronted him about the rape charge."

Sitting back she stared at the ceiling, her eyes beginning to sting. It was almost as if a weight had been lifted from her shoulders, yet, she couldn't shake the feeling that she'd made a mistake.

Detective Braum pulled her from her thoughts, "Miss Evans, would you like me to arrange some counselling sessions for you?" Seeing her expression, he quickly defended himself, "I don't mean to offend, it's just that… maybe your paranoia and worry surrounding George is just a manifestation of the fact that you haven't fully processed losing your parents yet?"

"Excuse me? I'm…" Nicola wanted to argue, but quickly realised that maybe he had a point. Surely it couldn't be healthy that some days she tried to get by pretending that nothing had happened at all. Other days the magnitude of what had happened hit her out of nowhere, "That might not be a bad idea."

Braum smiled reassuringly at her and reached into his desk, retrieving a rectangular white strip of card, "This is the number of one of the best therapists I've ever worked with. She works with people like you. People that have experienced great loss and trauma. Please just take it, even if you don't use it."

Nicola nodded as she reached for the card, "Can she help cure my memory loss? That would sure be helpful right about now!" She scoffed and shook her head.

He spoke again, softer this time – almost kind, "Miss Evans? The other night in my office. How did you know about Stephanie?"

She sank further into her seat, awkwardly playing with her hands. Finally she made eye contact with him, "Well, when I was in the hospital, I got talking to…" She paused, deciding whether or not to bring Rosemary up, "…one of the nurses. They told me why you are the way you are."

He raised his eyebrows, then nodded, seeming shocked at the comment.

"Oh, I didn't mean that the way it sounded. I should never have brought it up, I know that. I was just so angry and defensive but…I know that's no excuse."

She looked down at her hands and he sighed.

He knew exactly where she got the information from, "You were talking to Rosie weren't you?"

Nicola's eyes drifted back up to his, confusion in her face, "I'm sorry…who?"

Braum looked over at her from his chair, "Rosemary? That used to be my little nickname for her." He rolled his eyes, "Oh I suppose you'll find out sooner or later. Rosie and I were married; Stephanie was our daughter."

Nicola nodded, still unsure of how much knowledge she should reveal – she knew this, but should she admit it? Rosemary had warned her that he was very private about Stephanie.

To her surprise, he continued, "After what happened I just… I became obsessed. I closed myself off. I suppose after a while it was just too much and she left me. Every time I see her, I can't believe what I lost…" He trailed off, clearing his throat.

Nicola tried to hide the pity she felt for him, knowing that he was not the kind of person that wanted to be seen as weak, "I'm so sorry. Have you tried to talk to her about it? Rosemary is wonderful. I'm sure she forgives you."

"Oh, I don't know. She was grieving, and I wasn't there for her."

"But you still care for each other. I could see it that night in the hospital."

"I don't know about all that. I'm just saying…use me as an example of how you *don't* want to be. Not processing your grief will tear you up eventually."

She wasn't sure how to respond but before she could, he stood up, "I'll get someone to take you home now." She nodded in response as he ushered her towards the door, signaling to this closest officer with a wave of his hand.

9

Several days had passed since Nicola's impromptu therapy session with Braum.

Rosemary and Braum… she knew there had to be something there with the way they looked at each other that night in the hospital. With the way that Rosemary spoke about him. It was so obvious. She couldn't imagine the trauma of losing a child – losing her parents was bad enough! The damage it must have done to their relationship was fixable – she just knew it.

Speaking of, her mind drifted to George. She had no idea if they'd taken him in or not. Things were unusually quiet.

"Hello? Are you in there, sweetheart?" The soft rasp of Rosemary's voice entwined with her light taps on the door.

She couldn't help but smile as she called back, "Yeah, I'll be right there!"

Nicola swung open the door and Rosemary immediately enveloped her in a bear hug, "So, where are we going today? My treat!" Nicola began to protest, but Rosemary simply held up her hand, "No discussion. It's my treat."

She knew that Rosemary wouldn't take no for an answer; she was far too stubborn for that, "Let's go shopping. I could do with some new shoes."

"That's better. Let's go. We're wasting valuable shopping time."

***

By the third shop, Nicola's feet were tender from all the shoes she'd forced on, but she didn't want to stop. This was a nice distraction from the craziness of her life. She couldn't remember the last time she'd relaxed and just let her guard down.

"Hey, Rosemary? I know I probably shouldn't

mention this and it's none of my business…"

Rosemary turned to look at her, "What isn't your business, sweetie?"

"I was talking to Detective Braum and he mentioned, well, he told me a little bit about you two. It sounds like you were really happy for a long time."

Rosemary smiled, "He's right. We were happily married for 30 years."

Nicola just stared and Rosemary laughed, "Sure, he's always been a very private man but with me, with Stephanie, he was more loving and sweeter than any man I'd ever known. It broke my heart the day he was served with the divorce papers. I still love him."

Nicola put her hand on Rosemary's shoulder, "He still loves you, you know? I can tell."

"Well, I just don't know if I agree with you about that. He's not exactly easy for me to read, and I was *married* to him!" She looked over at Nicola, "Are you ok? You seem a bit pre-occupied today?"

Picking up yet another pair of black stilettos Nicola smiled, trying her best to make it seem genuine, "Well, not really. Something happened with George."

"What do you mean?"

"When I was back at the house doing the walkthrough, I saw someone watching me from outside the window. I didn't see their face, but I got a glimpse of their build and what they were wearing." She took a deep breath before continuing, "Later on, I went to George's and found clothes that looked exactly like the ones that the man outside the house was wearing." Rosemary couldn't hide her shock, but Nicola carried on, "So, I confronted him about it, and about a charge that Detective Braum told me about. I mean, he didn't deny any of it. He just seemed confused about the whole thing and I didn't know what to do so I went to the station and told Braum."

Rosemary was about to speak but was cut off when she rounded the corner, bumping into someone.

Before she fell, a large arm reached out to steady her, "I'm so sorry, are you ok?"

Brushing loose strands of hair back from her face and

straightening her bag, she nodded, "Oh yes, I'm quite alright thank you."

Nicola came to her defence, immediately squaring her shoulders, ready for a fight. That was until she saw who they'd bumped into, "Ethan?"

She was greeted by a wide grin, a complete shift to the look she'd received last time she saw him. He took a second and then managed to find his voice, "Hey...Nicola, right?"

"Care to introduce me?" Rosemary chimed in.

Nicola shook her head, "Oh, sorry! This is Ethan, he's George's roommate. Ethan, this is Rosemary. She looked after me in the hospital."

"Hi Ethan," Rosemary offered with a smile, "Actually, I think we've met before."

He stiffened at the suggestion and then painted on a friendly smile, "No I, uh...I don't think so. I'm pretty sure I'd remember such a lovely lady."

Nicola couldn't believe how charismatic he was being; especially with how he was during their first meeting.

Rosemary didn't even register the compliment, "I'm pretty sure we have," She clicked her fingers together, "That's right, at the hospital," she added. "You were assisting Dr Jeffries weren't —"

He cut her off, "No, I think you're mistaken." Almost as if he'd realised that he'd spoken out of turn, he let out a nervous laugh, "I'm sorry. Where are my manners? It's nice to meet you, Rosemary. Sorry about running into you. I wasn't paying attention."

Tilting her head slightly, Nicola narrowed her eyes at him, momentarily taken aback with the assertive tone he'd used with Rosemary. Like he was trying to find a way to make her stop talking.

Rosemary, on the other hand, didn't show any concern. She simply smiled at him, a hardness in her eyes, "Hmm... How odd. I'm usually great at remembering faces, but I guess I must be mistaken."

Ethan turned to Nicola, "Hey, how're you holding up? I heard the police were holding George?"

Her stomach dropped as soon as she heard his name,

"Were they? I didn't even know. Here," she motioned to the indoor café, "let's have a coffee." Once they'd ordered Nicola couldn't help herself, she had to ask, "How's he doing?" No matter what he might have done, she still cared about him.

Ethan shuffled in his seat, shrugging his shoulders, "I honestly don't know. I haven't seen him in a few days."

"What do you mean? You live with him?"

"He came home two days ago, after talking to that Detective, and said he needed a break. Took some of his things and that's the last I've heard from him."

"Interesting, how long have you known George, Ethan?" Rosemary questioned.

"Well, I met him, well, it must have been over ten years ago now. We've always been quite good buddies, dipping in and out of each other's lives, you know?"

"Wow, that's quite a while. So surely you know whether or not he's capable of hurting anyone?"

Ethan seemed to smirk and looked down at his coffee, "I don't know. They say it's always the quiet ones you have to watch, right? I mean who knows what anyone is really capable of?"

Rosemary turned to Nicola, "Oh, come on, Nicola. You can't be serious? Do you honestly believe that George could do something like that? Murder your parents and hold you hostage in your own basement?" When she didn't respond, Rosemary carried on, "Let's face it, someone would have to be incredibly unhinged in the first place to do such horrible things."

Nicola shook her head and shrugged her shoulders as she replied, "I don't know. It doesn't make any sense! There's so much going on right now and after what Detective Braum told me, all I know is that I've got to keep myself safe."

There was something in Nicola's gut telling her that she was wrong to suspect George, but she couldn't risk trusting it. What if she was wrong… *again*?

She quickly blinked away the tears beginning to form in her eyes as she stood up from the table, "I'm just going to the bathroom for a second."

As she walked away, her mind was racing. She was furious at herself…at her memory, or lack, thereof! She

53

couldn't understand why more of her memories weren't coming back. *Why can't you remember that night?*

Rubbing her forehead, she sighed, "Well that was rude, Nicola." She turned, wanting to apologise for effectively running away from the table. *Oh, what's going on?* She thought to herself as she watched Rosemary and Ethan converse; there was clearly some kind of tension between the two of them.

Her senses heightened as Ethan stood, towering over Rosemary. He quickly glanced at Nicola as she walked back to the table, then turned and left.

"What the hell was that about, Rosemary?"

"I don't like that boy, Nicola. He's been friends with George for ten years and seems to have no idea of his character…his true nature? Instead of defending him, he almost seemed to condemn him."

"Yeah, that did look a bit heated."

"He just really gives me the heebie jeebies, Nicola. I don't trust that boy. There's something about him but I just can't put my finger on it."

In an attempt to distract her from whatever uncomfortable conversation had just happened between them, Nicola spoke quickly, "Come on, don't let him ruin our day. Let's get shopping, we're losing daylight."

10

"I will, don't worry." Rosemary laughed in disbelief as she walked to the door of the apartment, "Gosh, I'm supposed to be worried about you. Not the other way around."

Nicola smiled reassuringly, "You don't have to worry about me; I'm ok." She sensed a protest threatening to surface as they embraced, so she quickly added, "You know I appreciate it though. Now go on or you'll be late. Don't forget, I want a call when you get home.'

There was one final smile and wave, and then Rosemary was gone.

As she closed the door behind her, Nicola smiled. It had only been a week but her evenings of wine and food with Rosemary had quickly replaced her evenings with George and, although she was thankful for the distraction, she couldn't help missing him. She still hadn't heard from him since the police questioned him, which made her uneasy, but her worries were calmed by the fact that Jones was stationed on the street below the apartment in his patrol car, having taken over from the previous officer.

Looking out onto the dark street, she noticed that there appeared to be no one actually in said car. Jones was gone. *Maybe he's getting a coffee,* she rationalized, forgetting about the fact that most coffee shops closed by 6p.m. Shrugging her shoulders, she flopped onto the sofa and turned up the volume.

The *'Ghost Adventures'* team were about to begin their lockdown in the Sacramento Tunnels when Nicola's mobile phone rang. She didn't look at the caller ID, worried that she'd miss a key bit of evidence on the show. Putting the phone to her ear, she spoke, "Hello?"

There was a muffled noise and Nicola's back straightened. Her body always seemed to know when there was something wrong. Sitting forward in her seat, she asked again more sternly, "Hello?"

"Miss Evans… you… it's... Braum..."

"Detective? I can barely hear you. The reception isn't very good!" She lowered the volume on the T.V., hoping it would help.

"Sorry, Miss Evans, can you hear me now? I was going through the tunnel. Where are you?"

"I'm at the apartment, why?"

"OK, I need you to stay there and make sure the door is bolted. Don't let anyone in until I get there, do you understand me?"

Nicola's palms began to sweat and her heart rate increased as she stood and moved towards the door, "What's going on?"

He must have been going through another tunnel because she could barely hear him, "... neighbours... apartment... payphone..."

Just as she pulled the chain across the door, the apartment phone started ringing. Without even thinking, she responded to Braum, "Just one second. The other phone is going now!"" She picked up the receiver, "Hello?"

Nothing. Silence. Letting her frustration show, Nicola moved to hang up when she caught a glimpse out the corner of her eye. Something moving on the dark, empty street outside.

Peeking out of the window, she noticed a shape. She kept staring at it, hoping that it would move again so that she could put her irrational fears to bed. Next to the payphone across the street, was a man dressed in dark clothes. He had a cap on, so Nicola couldn't see his face, but she didn't have to. Her body knew that something was wrong, the pit in her stomach confirming what the hairs on the back of her neck were once again telling her.

He stared up at her, receiver in hand, for what felt like an eternity before putting the phone down. Nicola wanted to believe it was just a coincidence, but the fact that the line went dead on her end at the exact same time cemented the obvious.

He crossed the street. Towards the apartment building.

"Braum?! Braum, he's here! He's coming up to my apartment! Braum?"

He coughed, his voice raspy from calling out to her,

"Hide. Make sure the door is locked and hide. I'm almost there!"

Nicola tried to hang up the call, but her hands were shaking so much that she couldn't. She threw the phone down on the couch and ran to the bedroom.

It didn't occur to her until after she began hearing noises near the front door, that she was hiding in the same spot as before. In the most obvious of spaces.

Under her bed.

***

When Detective Braum arrived, his fear was realised. Nicola was gone.

"Why was no one watching her?! Where's Jones?"

A young officer entered the room, trying to hold back her heaves, "Sir? You'd better come outside. We've found Jones."

Detective Braum couldn't believe it. There was his partner for over 5 years. Contrary to Nicola's belief, Jones was still in the car, with the seatbelt tightly wound around his torso keeping him upright. Detective Braum made his way to the front of the patrol car. There were multiple stab wounds in Jones' chest – probably inflicted from behind – and a deep wound in his throat.

"Son of a bitch!" Braum gritted through his teeth, running a hand through his tangled hair, and pacing back and forth. He turned to the officers, "What the hell happened here?!" Their blank stares infuriated him, "Get back up there and tell me where this bastard has taken her!"

As the officers scurried away, their tales between their legs, Braum leant on the front of the car. He couldn't help but feel guilt. He wasn't there to protect her; to watch out for Jones.

He felt so helpless.

It was like Stephanie all over again.

***

The back of Nicola's head stung. She didn't know

what she'd been hit with, but boy did it hurt! Her lips were dry. She licked them and tasted iron – blood. She opened her eyes, but the darkness didn't lift. After a few seconds, she worked out that she had a bag over her head. She struggled, trying to move, but she couldn't. She was tied to something; it felt like a chair. Suddenly, the bag was ripped from her head and she could see again – barely. The only light came from candles placed around the room.

Panting but not wanting to show weakness, she looked around the room defiantly, "Oh come on. Surely you don't need to hide from a helpless girl tied to a chair?" There was no response, so she pushed further, "Oh don't be shy. George? We both know how this is gonna go, don't we? Detective Braum is probably on his way here right now and—"

She was cut off by a low laugh that seemed to echo around the room; her eyes darting all over as she tried to find the source.

"Oh, Nicola..." Her back stiffened, recognising the voice.

"Ethan?"

11

Braum couldn't sit still. He paced back and forth across his office trying to think of some way, anyway, to find Nicola.

He was determined that this time would be different; he was determined not to fail Nicola like he did Stephanie. That's all it took. One little thought and he was right back there. To the last time that he saw Stephanie.

He was sat in his favourite armchair going through unsolved case files. His version of relaxation!

A creak in the hallway caught his attention, turning him away from the grizzly photographs arranged on his lap. Rosemary was pulling a double at work, so it had to be Stephanie.

His police instinct kicking in, he slowly stood and moved to the door, shrouded in the darkness from the hallway.

Sure enough, Stephanie was creeping down the stairs. The smell of the perfume they'd bought her three Christmases ago hit his nostrils and he was momentarily transported back to when she was little. Still his little girl.

She reached the bottom of the stairs and he flicked the light switch, clearly catching her by surprise.

"Dad! What are you doing creeping around in the dark?! I thought you were in bed."

"I could ask you the same question. Where are you going at this time of night...?" It was then that he realised she was wearing more makeup than usual, and that she was dressed a little...out of character, "Or more to the point; where are you going looking like that?"

Stephanie stumbled on her words, trying to hide the fact that she hadn't thought of a cover story. She obviously didn't plan on getting caught! "Well, I just...there's a few of us girls just getting together over at Amy's house and you know - it's kind of like a little party. Nothing exciting or anything, just a few kids from school." She said it almost as a question,

*furrowing her brows and nervously awaiting her father's
response.*

*He nodded, clearly weighing up her story before
responding, "Hmm... well you're not going over there looking
like that."*

*"What do you mean? What's wrong with how I
look!"*

*"Really? You're wearing eighteen layers of makeup,
and," He pointed at her legs, "is that a skirt, or a belt? So
obviously there are going to be boys there. I'm not an idiot
and, as much as you seem to think so, I wasn't born
yesterday." Before she had a chance to complain, he
continued, "so you'd better just go upstairs and re-think the
situation. You're not going looking like that."*

*"I'm not a little girl anymore. You can't keep me
locked up in here forever!" Stephanie shouted as she stormed
back up the stairs; Braum following close behind.*

*"Don't you walk away from me when I'm talking to
you!" He grabbed her arm and spun her around, "I'm not
stupid. There will be boys and drinking; you're too young.
Don't you know what could happen? I see it all the time, day
in and day out. What people do to each other...I don't want
you to end up as one of my cases!"*

*She yanked her arm out of his grasp, cutting him off,
"Why not?! You'd see a hell of a lot more of me than you do
now if I was on a slab in the morgue! This is exactly what's
wrong! All you ever do is work! Even when you're home,
you're still there in your head. Are me and mum not enough
for you anymore?! Why can't you just be here with us?!"*

*Braum was stumped, "Baby, Stephanie you don't
understand."*

*Not breaking eye contact she slowly backed away
into her bedroom, her safe haven, "I can't wait to get out of
here. I hate you."*

Braum's phone buzzed on his desk, the vibrations
bringing him back to reality and away from the memory of his
daughter's face as she slammed the bedroom door.

If only he'd followed her in and tried to talk to her
instead of going back downstairs, pouring himself a whisky

and plugging back into those damn files. He might have stopped her sneaking out of the window and…

Shaking his head, as if to free himself from the haze, he answered the phone.

Rosemary spoke between panicked breaths, "John? I got your message. What's happened? Where is Nicola? Is she ok?"

He smoothed his hair with his hand, something he always did when he was nervous. A tick, you might say. "Rosie, calm down. We don't know all of the facts yet, so we can't be sure of what's happened."

"You said it looked like there was a struggle at her place, right? Oh God… what if that psycho found her? She thought she was being followed for a while, but I just put it down to post-traumatic stress or something. If I'd known she was right, I would've done something. I would've…I don't know but I wouldn't have just ignored it!"

Braum steadied his voice trying to form a firm, yet soft, response, "Rosie, please. As of right now, I just want to find her before something bad happens. I want to find her before it's too late, again…" He trailed off to the sound of her sniffling.

"John, listen to me. What happened to Stephanie was not your fault. You couldn't have known what was going to happen."

"I need you to think, Rosie. Are there any places that she might have gone to if she was in trouble? Anywhere she would go to in an emergency."

There was a slight pause before she answered, "I don't know. I would have thought that if she was in trouble, she'd either go to you or me!"

"Where are you?"

"I'm at the hospital, working. Why?"

Braum threw on his jacket as he replied, "Just…stay there. I need to know that at least one person is safe tonight. I have to go back out and search, but I'll swing by the hospital once I'm done."

"Oh, John, you don't have to do that honestly."

"I know I don't, Rosie. I want to." Before he could talk himself out of it, he found the words escaping the vault that he'd kept closed for so long, "I miss you."

He could sense the smile in her voice, reminding him of the good times, "I miss you too."

He paused and then hung up, realising that he'd already lost one of the most important people to him. He was not about to lose another one. "Let's go, guys! You're not going to catch him sitting at your desks!" He walked through the station with a purpose. Tonight, he was going to save a life.

12

"Bingo! She finally gets it!" Ethan laughed again as he emerged from the shadows to her right.

Nicola looked around the room, confusion swirling in her mind, "Why are there candles in here? Have you been working with George all this time? I don't under—"

Ethan's boots made a thunderous noise as he crossed the distance between them, now face to face with her. So close that she could smell his breath, his aftershave. *Cinnamon?*

"George, George, George! Is he all you talk about? No, ok? For your information, perfect Georgie…" He moved over to a doorway and pulled out another chair. This one wasn't empty either. It contained a seemingly lifeless body, the head leaning forwards at an almost-inhuman angle and the arms hanging loosely despite being tied. Nicola saw the beard and realised almost immediately that it was George, "What have you done?" She struggled against her restraints, trying to cross the distance between them.

Ethan continued, ignoring her completely, "…For once, he isn't the center of attention. He isn't a part of this. He isn't the golden boy! I mean, honestly. Look at him," He grabbed a fist-full of George's hair, roughly pulling his head backwards, "Do you really think he could pull this off? Sweet, loveable George?"

She couldn't grasp what was right in front of her, "I don't understand. What are you…" All at once, it dawned on her. Everything made sense. All of the clues fit together like the pieces of a clever puzzle, "So…wait, it was you who broke in that night and…" Her voice trailed off; she couldn't finish the sentence.

With surprising confidence, Ethan spoke, "Yep." He smiled, his face contorting as he crouched down in front of her. Nicola tried to push herself backwards, but Ethan stopped her by holding onto her thighs. Shrugging his shoulders, he said, "I mean I have to admit, killing your parents wasn't exactly part of the plan."

"Why...?" Nicola's voice trailed into silence.

"Oh, no pillow talk? You want to get straight into it? Ok here we go. Are you comfy?"

She narrowed her eyes at him, waiting for him to carry on.

"Believe it or not, I've not always been the amazing man that I am today. I got into a little bit of trouble when I was younger. Fell in with the wrong crowd, you might say. Long story short, after a few years of stealing from my *sickeningly* wealthy parents, they kicked me out – said they didn't want anything to do with me anymore. So, I did what any abandoned, mistreated child would do," He bopped her on the nose and grinned, "I started planning! I mean, it didn't end so well for them. What with them dying in that car accident." He looked at Nicola, relishing every ounce of disgust and hatred she had for him at that moment, "I know*! How does nobody know*? Well, I'm a *very* good actor and moving away helped. Hey - this ain't my first rodeo."

"You're insane. Let me out of here or I swear to God—"

Ethan moved closer, getting right in her face, "Don't interrupt me again."

She gulped and sat backwards in her chair, trying to move away from the hand that was stroking her face.

Moving her hair behind her ears and noticing the pink scar on her cheek, a grotesque smile crept across his face, "Oh yes. I forgot. I certainly made a mark on you, didn't I? I didn't want to do that, you know?" He stared at her, seemingly lost in thought, "You just had to push me though, didn't you? I do wish I'd gone for something a bit less horrid, though. I mean…a bite? It seemed like a good idea at the time but…it has ruined your beautiful face just a tad, hasn't it?!"

Nicola held back tears as he snapped out of his trance and took a deep breath, "Where was I? Oh yeah! The tragic, *accidental* death of my parents. Afterwards, I had to keep moving around and that's when I met George. He was easy to manipulate because he's…well, he's weak, isn't he?"

Nicola noticed that he kept rubbing her legs as he spoke.

"Anyway, I owed a lot of money to some really bad

people. Obviously poor, innocent George never knew anything about that. I personally think I deserve an Oscar for my performance there." He paused as if waiting for applause and when none came, he carried on, "So, I couldn't get the money from George because he's pretty much broke, but I knew I could get it quickly if I broke into the right house and so it had to be one of the houses on your street. I mean, come on! It *is* one of the wealthiest streets in town! Sucks for you though, I suppose."

She scoffed.

He shrugged his shoulders, "I decided that your parents' house was the one for me! But when I saw you come outside in those tight, green leggings with your hair down and curly, I knew I wanted something other than expensive watches, jewellery and T.V. sets. You were just… you were beautiful." As he cleared his throat, Nicola tried to hold back the urge to vomit, "Anyway, I'm getting off-topic here. I picked my night and went for it! Of course, your parents decided to ruin it. It would've been perfect if your dad hadn't come downstairs and caught me." Ethan took a deep breath to calm himself, "Although, I suppose in the end it was a good thing. It meant that we had a couple of days to ourselves in that roomy basement of theirs."

He looked up at her expectantly and she coughed back vomit as she responded, "So…so my parents were murdered because you were too scared to face the *wrong people*?!"

Ethan narrowed his eyes at her and then chuckled, "I know what you're trying to do. You're trying to distract me, but it won't work. Surely you must remember how great the basement was?"

"I… uh… I don't remember."

"Oh, that doesn't matter, I'll be happy to remind you later, when we get rid of George."

Nicola's stomach dropped as she peered over Ethan's massive shoulders to George. He still hadn't moved, and Nicola feared the worst. Through the veil of concern, she heard Ethan speak again but zoned out. She was more focused on George; silently willing him to move.

Ethan circled her, "I'll never forget when they took

you from me. I was coming back from a supply run and saw them taking you out of the house and putting you into an ambulance. I was furious that they'd interrupted our time together… until I noticed where the ambulance was from. That's how I knew that me finding you was fate. They were taking you to Maple Blossom General, where I was assisting a doctor. If that isn't fate, then I don't know what is!"

She felt a sting across her cheek and stared at Ethan in shock, "Do I have your attention now? What the hell were you looking at?!" He glanced over his shoulder and laughed.

Looking back at Nicola through hooded eyes, he nodded and stood up, "What a surprise... little George. You know, this guy has always been the favourite. We were like brothers for ten years. For ten years, I was overshadowed by the golden boy." He moved behind George but kept eye contact with Nicola. "I take it you heard about his rape charge then?" He drank in the sight of Nicola stiffening at the word, "Oh, yes. I'll bet that's why you were arguing that day. Would you like the full story? I'm guessing the cops didn't fill in the blanks for you?"

She glared at him, but quickly covered it with a forced smile. She couldn't risk pushing him over the edge with George there; she didn't know what he would do, "I want to hear more. Please just, just come back over here and I swear I'll be completely focused?"

He smirked, "I'm fine here, thanks."

Stretching his neck and shoulders until they cracked and the veins bulged, he spoke again, "It all happened one night in college. Our house was hosting some stupid frat Halloween party and it was my perfect opportunity to take away our little golden boy's high status. To bring him back down to Earth, so to speak. I was so tired of being pushed aside for everything; girls, class, friends – all because of him! I just had to find the perfect way to do it. Enter; incredibly drunk girl - you know, I don't even remember her name - and a plan. All of us were wearing the same stupid costume – a small toga thinly draped over us with our big, bulging muscles on show and a full mask. So, she didn't even see my face. I just asked if she wanted a little fun and of course, she was more than happy to oblige."

"I don't want to hear this."

"Sorry princess, but it's key to the story. Anyway, we did the deed, safely of course, I'm not an idiot. Although I did have to assert some dominance and remind her that she wanted it halfway through. The stupid bitch changed her mind and said no to me. Can you believe that? No... to me! Then it hit me. Would she say no to precious Georgie?"

Nicola turned her face away and bit back tears, "Stop. Please."

Ethan appeared unmoved by her tears, "So, I just had to finish the plan. It was simple really; find George, get him drunk, take him up to the room, pull down his Calvins, put him on top of her and boom!" He clapped his hands together and delved deeper into the story, "I mean, drunk girls at these parties always regret it the next day, don't they? They're all rich girls that will tell dear old daddy anything to stay 'daddy's little girl' capable of inheriting! What a crime!" He moved towards her, arms outstretched and smiling, like some kind of twisted ringmaster.

Nicola was tired of his arrogance. Looking him dead in the eye, she spoke, "Didn't turn out so well though did it? I mean, the charges were dropped, and he wasn't convicted. So really, you failed, didn't you? George won that one without even knowing he was playing."

Ethan nodded at her as he again crouched in front of her. He pouted his lips, pulling a knife from his waistband. She immediately stiffened as he lay the cold blade against her cheek, "Shall we put a scar on the other cheek? Maybe my name this time? So the world will really know you're mine?"

Nicola's eyes darted to George, her mind silently wishing for him to wake up and save her from Ethan's craziness.

"Oh no, wait... this is a much better plan!" He shouted, moving over to George and grabbing another fistful of his hair. He yanked his head back as he placed the blade to George's throat, "I guess I win this time."

George opened his eyes and grabbed Ethan's arm, holding it back and trying to keep the knife from his skin, "You can't tie a knot for shit, asshole!"

George threw his head sideways into Ethan's,

knocking him down, and wasted no time pushing his chair away. Making way for a fight. He stomped over to Ethan, his bulky shoulders squared, and threw him against the wall. A punch to the stomach, another headbutt, a kick and Ethan was down again.

George picked up the knife and moved to Nicola, "Here, let's get you out of these ropes, shall we?"

She cleared her throat, trying to steady her voice as George freed her arms, "I'm so sorry. I swear… I didn't know what to do."

He quickly hugged her and then pulled away. Nicola feared the worst; she feared that she had ruined what she and George had shared. That was until he kissed her, quick yet soft, "Stop apologising. We're ok, but our priority is getting out of here now."

Nicola looked around in confusion, "But where are we? I don't... I don't recognise..." Looking over George's shoulder, she noticed a glowing exit sign, "Wait… we must be in the hospital! The new section!"

"Let's get out of here and—" He was cut off when Ethan hooked his hands around his ankle and pulled him to the ground.

"George!"

"Nicola, go now! I'll be right behind you."

Even though she knew she should run and get help, she couldn't help but want to stay. Tearing up, she looked at George and shouted, "I'll get help! I'll bring someone."

She burst through the double doors and out into the corridor, not stopping until she reached the elevator. It took a few moments for Nicola to realise that the buttons weren't illuminated and that the strip at the top of the doors showed no numbers. *Damn it! Out of order!* Frantically searching for another option, she noticed a fire alarm hidden around the sidewall. She ran to it. If there wasn't power for the elevator, it would take a miracle for the fire alarm to be working, but she didn't care. She had to try the attract attention of the night shift staff working downstairs.

She pulled it.

***

Braum stared at the red lights, a row of cars lined up in front of him. There had been a sign a couple of miles back warning about traffic delays and construction, but he hadn't taken any notice of the date.

To his frustration, the officers back at Nicola's apartment hadn't found any trace at all. No hairs, no fibers...nothing. It was as if she'd been kidnapped by a ghost.

"Come on!" He slammed his fist into the steering wheel, wondering whether or not it would be worth using his lights and siren. After a few minutes, he decided against it. The hard shoulder was full of equipment so there was nowhere for anyone to go anyway.

"Is anyone on Cooper Street? I'm in traffic but I need someone at the hospital to check things out." A cacophony of "no's and apologies rang out over the radio. Braum shifted in his seat, his seatbelt tightening. He gripped the radio so hard, his hand cramped.

Finally, after what felt like an eternity, the row of cars in front of him began to move. He rolled to a stop a few hundred yards from where he'd started and found himself at the front of the queue of traffic, waiting for the lights to turn green. There was something going on; his gut told him that much, at least. He just didn't know what it was, "Come on, for Christ's sake! Change!"

As if it had been listening, the light changed to green and Braum moved through, ignoring the speed limit. He drove towards the hospital, trying to keep his thoughts positive. He needed to make sure Rosemary was safe, refusing to let himself think that she could be in danger.

He needed to find Nicola and quickly. The longer it took to find her, the greater the chance was that he'd be finding a body instead. Images of Stephanie's case file flashed through his mind, "Not this time." He said defiantly, stiffening his back and turning onto Cooper Street.

13

Rosemary carefully opened up the door to the security office and peered inside, "Hey fellas! Coffee break?"

The two men inside smiled and took their respective mugs from the tray.

"You're an angel in human form, Rosemary. Do you know that?" Ron chuckled playfully. He was in his fifties with thinning hair, but he had managed to maintain a physique to rival any bodybuilder. You could tell that he was a softy deep down; his coffee mug gave him away. It was plastered with printed photographs of smiling grandchildren and hyperactive pets.

Rosemary laughed and looked over at Al. He was a little younger - in his mid-40s - with a full head of hair and harsh features. All physical attributes aside, Al was just as kind as Ron but hid it a little better. His mug was quite plain, with a caricature of a middle finger gracing the front.

"You see, Al? That's how you get extra sugar in your coffee. Ron knows how to compliment a lady!"

The three of them laughed and sipped their coffees, trying to shake off the inevitable cobwebs of the dreaded night shift.

"So, is there anything interesting happening tonight then?"

"Nada," Al answered, blowing into his cup, "I swear, I don't think we're even needed at this time of night! Nothing ever happens."

Ron scoffed, "Please. You know if anything ever were to happen, you'd be the first one under that desk!"

They erupted into laughter but were quickly halted by Rosemary's next question.

"Hey, Ron?" Rosemary tapped him on the shoulder, "What's that light flashing for on your board? I thought that was for the new sections. They aren't open yet though, are they?"

Ron set down his coffee, "As far as I know, they

aren't up and running yet. I mean, a few doctors have started setting up their offices but they should all be gone by now."

"Looks like a fire alarm has been tripped. Tap into the CCTV, Ron. Just to make sure there are no racoons up there. Hell, for all we know, some Goddamn workers have gotten lost up there." Al always looked on the bright side.

The three of them watched the monitors for what seemed like an eternity, scanning for any sign of movement.

"Oh my God—" Al peered at the screen closer, "There's a girl up there. Is she…why is she running?"

"Wait, what?" Rosemary pulled her phone from her pocket and began calling Braum. Putting it to her ear, she looked at Ron and Al, "That's Nicola. The local girl that was attacked a while back and has just gone missing. The one my John is looking for?" She backed away from them, trying not to be distracted by their questions and escalating shouts of alarm.

He answered almost immediately, and she didn't give him a chance to speak, "John? She's here. I don't know how, and I don't know what's going on, but Nicola's here. She's on the upper floors; the new areas. We've just seen her on the CCTV. John, she's tripped a fire alarm and it looked like she was running away from something… or someone."

"Rosie, stay where you are. Do you hear me? Send the security guards up and tell them to take their firearms. Our guy could be there and should be considered armed and dangerous. I'm coming straight there but please stay out of the way. I don't want you putting yourself in danger."

"I'm ok, John. Ron and Al have already gone up there, but please just get here as soon as you can. I hate the idea of her running around up there with me just sitting here."

It had been around thirty minutes and no one had come back. No Ron, Al, Nicola or Braum. Rosemary not only grew restless, but also worried. Surely Ron and Al were able to handle whatever situation was going on? They were giants, for God's sake!

"That's it," she whispered to herself as she took one last look at the clock and left the staff room. It looked like the elevator was having some repair work done, so Rosemary pushed open the door to the stairwell and started up.

***

Nicola had lost count of how many corners she'd taken, and how many corridors she'd crept through. She didn't know how long it had been since she'd activated the fire alarm and in truth, she didn't even know if it had worked.

Hearing movement a few steps behind and, deciding to err on the side of caution, she ducked into an empty room and hid out of sight of the clear windows not yet covered with blinds. After a few moments, she risked a glance at the glass and saw a tall, broad shape quickly pass by. Forced backwards out of sight by her own fear, Nicola found herself silently doing something she hadn't done in a long time; praying.

"Nicola?"

The whisper was so quiet, she wasn't sure she'd actually heard it at all.

"Oh God, please be in here… Nicola?" There it was again, closer this time and the voice sounded familiar.

Bracing herself, Nicola peered around the corner and almost wept with relief as Rosemary snuck into the room. She had never been so happy to see anyone, yet at the same time been so worried about someone's safety.

"Rosemary?" she whispered back. "Over here. Quick, come here."

When they were safely blocked from view, Rosemary hugged Nicola and checked her over, noticing the red marks forming over the bruises beginning to fade on her wrists, "Oh my God, Nicola. You're ok! Wait, what are these? We need to get you downstairs. Come on."

Nicola waved her hands at Rosemary, not realising how much they were shaking. She tried to slow her breathing enough to speak, her heart beating so loudly it was the only thing she could hear, "Rosemary…Rosemary, he did it. He killed my parents! We just…we need to be quiet. I don't know where he is, but we can't let him find us!"

Rosemary's eyes widened as she put her hands onto Nicola's shoulders. She spoke quietly, cutting through the panicked breathing filling the air, "What do you mean? Who killed them? Nicola, who can't find us? What are you talking about?"

"Ethan. You were right, Rosemary. I'm so sorry that I didn't listen when you tried to warn me. He took me and George...he's been acting out some sick game up here."

Rosemary rubbed Nicola's shoulders to calm her, "Ethan did all this? So was he the one that murdered your parents as well?" Nicola answered with a slight nod, "Wait, you said that George is here too? Where is he?"

At the mention of George's name, tears fell freely from Nicola's eyes. Her breathing quickened and her chest tightened at the thought that George might have been hurt, "I have no idea if he's ok or not. He was fighting with Ethan and told me to run... I was trying to get help, but I couldn't find the stairs."

"Well, I got up here using the stairs so we can get out the same way. Ron and Al, our security guys, are up here now, so they'll deal with Ethan and I'm sure they'll find George. John is on his way and for now, we just need to get downstairs, ok?"

She didn't want to leave without George, but she had to believe Rosemary. After all, what could she do to help him? She was powerless against Ethan's size and bulk!

They crept to the door and steadied themselves for the journey to the stairwell. The corridor looked clear and they nodded to one another, sliding from the room and into the shadows.

"Almost there," Rosemary mouthed. Nicola slipped on the floor and reached to balance herself on Rosemary's arm. She looked down, finding her shoes sliding in a pool of dark red. She gasped as she grabbed Rosemary's arm tighter, "Oh, God. It's blood." Rosemary peered further down the hallway and then shifted back towards Nicola; her skin beaded with sweat, tinging with gray while her eyes widened into darkened rounds, "Nicola. It's the security guards, they are hurt. I need to check them, ok?"

Nicola nodded, her body ice cold.

They paused and then with shallow breaths, and with Nicola's legs shaking so hard they could barely hold her up, they crept towards the injured men. Nicola couldn't watch as Rosemary bent down to feel for pulses.

"Ron's still breathing."

Nicola looked closer, in surprise. There was so much blood. Memories of her mother lying in a pool of her own blood made her head pound.

"Ron! Hang in there. You're too big for me to carry, just please stay until help arrives." Rosemary picked up his hand and directed it to the wound, "Put pressure on this. Don't you give up on me!" Nicola pulled on Rosemary's arm and urged her to stand, "We need to keep moving. We can get help for him when we are downstairs." The threat of the man stalking her down the hallway caused a swell of bile to rise in her throat, "Come, Rosemary."

As they rounded the last corner, they slammed straight into Ethan, "Oh no you don't." He grabbed Rosemary and pushed Nicola backwards into the wall. He stared straight at Nicola and asked, "Where are you going? We're not finished."

"Ethan please… please just let her go and we... we can leave together. Right now?"

Narrowing his eyes at her, he smiled, "Now, why don't I believe you?" He turned his attention to Rosemary and looked down at her as he spoke, "Dear, sweet Rosemary. Why couldn't you just keep your nose out?" Ethan's voice trailed off as he pulled his knife from the waistband of his jeans. Nicola immediately moved forward, but he mirrored her speed, putting the knife up to Rosemary's throat, "Oh, I wouldn't do that, if I were you, Nicola. You don't want me to hurt her, now do you?" When she didn't respond he smirked and whispered into Rosemary's ear, "Where were we? Ah yes, you were trying to take Nicola away from me, weren't you?"

"Ethan, please!" Nicola screamed.

"Beg."

"What?" Nicola couldn't understand what was happening. He'd truly lost it, but she wasn't about to cost Rosemary her life. Swallowing her pride, she stared back at him defiantly, "Please don't hurt her. I'm begging you, Ethan."

He took a deep breath, his handsome face curled into a grotesque grin, "Mhmm. It's almost like music to my ears hearing that. Too bad that she tried to force us apart, isn't it? Sorry, Rosemary. You should've stayed out of it." His gaze shifted back up to meet Nicola's. He winked.

Nicola saw it all play out in slow motion. Before she could react, he plunged the knife into Rosemary's stomach; all the way to the hilt and laughed as she slowly slid to the floor.

"NO!" It was like being in a dream. Nicola heard the screaming but didn't realise it was coming from her. She finally stopped when the pain in her throat became too much.

"Nicola…run…" Rosemary choked out as she rolled onto her back and stared at the ceiling. She grabbed the bottom of her tunic and used it to apply pressure to the wound.

Nicola looked up at Ethan, her face painted with horror. Whimpers and panicked breathing again filled the air. Ethan's grin had spread into clown territory, almost comical if it weren't for the circumstances. For the second time that night, she turned and ran.

"Oh, Nicola. Why are you fighting this? Come on, don't make me chase you again!" He called out behind her, taunting and slow.

She tried every door handle on her way down the corridor, but they refused to open. *Oh God, please help me.* She could almost feel Ethan hot on her heels. Looking up, her mouth fell open. A dead end. There was nowhere left to go. She couldn't go forward…and she definitely couldn't go back.

"Well isn't this funny?" Ethan laughed, low and predatory. A shiver crept up Nicola's spine.

Turning to face him she saw that he still held the knife, dripping with blood. Rosemary's blood. She closed her eyes and took a deep breath, preparing herself for whatever was to come. Ethan crossed the distance between them and took Nicola in his arms.

"Get…off…me." Nicola swiped a hand across Ethan's face. She wasn't so lucky with the next blow; he saw it coming and blocked it. Staring down at her with desire and madness in his eyes, he breathed her name into her face and shoved her backwards, pushing her off balance.

Nicola didn't even need to see the blood; she just felt the sting as her head hit something hard. She turned to look at whatever she'd hit. Her fingers searched for the wound on her scalp, finally feeling the shape of the corner from the toolbox she'd landed on.

Hearing footsteps, she clawed her way to face them. The last thing she saw as her vision slowly closed in, was Ethan walking towards her. A sadistic grin on his face.

***

Braum took a deep breath and drew his weapon as he opened the stairwell door. He'd already called for back-up and hoped that they'd be joining him sooner rather than later. "Nicola? Talk to me! Where are you?" He was met with silence and whispered to himself, "We're doing this the hard way then I take it?"

As he slowly made his way through the maze of corridors Braum reacted to every noise, every shadow he saw. The corridors were silent save for the squeak of his shoes against the hardwood floor. Sweat began to bead on his brow as he turned a corner to his left, almost tripping over the security guards. He bent down and checked for a pulse. It was too late for one of them, but the other one seemed to have a faint beat, "Hang in there, big guy. Help is coming." He whispered as he looked around, inspecting the area for immediate threat. That's when he heard it. Was it a cough? A gargle? He pointed his gun in the direction of the sound and moved forwards, "Hey! If there's someone there, you'd better speak right now! Police!"

Braum moved further into the more well-lit area of the space and was sure he felt his heart actually break, "Rosie? Rosie, what the hell?" He rushed over to her, all the while keeping his gun drawn and ready to fire. When he reached her, he collapsed to his knees and cradled her in his arms, "Rosie, speak to me, please. You can't do this to me. You can't leave me! I'm not losing you again." He lay her down and checked for a pulse; it was only slight, but it was there.

He had a choice to make; Rosemary or Nicola.

"God forgive me," He whispered as he picked Rosemary's limp body up from the floor. She was unconscious and he wasn't taking any chances. He would come back for Nicola. He just hoped that he wouldn't be too late.

14

"Hey! Hey, I need someone over here," Braum burst through the double doors, "We've got a stab victim over here with a deep wound to the stomach, she needs help!"

Once they realised who he was holding in his arms, a swarm of nurses crowded and a gurney appeared. Braum lay Rosemary down and watched as they whisked her away.

He didn't notice the young nurse speaking to him until she gently put her hand on his shoulder, "Excuse me, sir? Come with me. We need to get you checked out."

He looked down at his blood-stained shirt, "Oh, it's... it's not mine, it's..." He couldn't finish, "I have to call this in, I'm sorry. We've still got a missing girl and a perp up there." He broke away from the nurse and spoke into his radio, "This is Detective Braum. Where is the back-up I ordered?"

A voice on the other end responded, "Sir, we're a bit thin on the ground tonight. I've rounded up everyone that is available and they are on their-"

He cut them off, "Hey, don't talk, just listen. I still need help. I'm going back in, so just get here now!"

Putting his radio back on his belt and drawing out his weapon again, Braum ran through the crowd now beginning to form and headed for the stairwell. He prepared himself with a few deep breaths and slipped back into the shadows of the new floor for what he hoped would be the last time.

After what felt like an hour of searching, Braum finally found an unlocked room. He slowly pushed open the door, keeping his gun aimed and ready to shoot, "Nicola? Are you in here?" He peered around inside the room, trying to distinguish shapes. There were candles set up around the room, though all but a couple had burnt out. Taking a chance, he flicked on his flashlight. In the corner, he noticed two legs sticking out from behind a desk, and there was a large pool of blood that must have been forming for quite some time. Slowly, he walked closer to the desk and looked over the edge, "George?" he muttered as he holstered his gun.

He still didn't trust George – not with that rape charge.

Braum didn't know what had happened but one thing was certain – he was hurt pretty badly, "Oh hell," He muttered as he spoke into his radio, "This is the situation. We have two injured parties up here, just across from the stairwell. One on the floor and one in the first room to the left, the only unlocked room it seems. We also have a missing girl up here and God knows who else. Keep alert." Moving through the maze of corridors, Braum slowly started to lose hope and decided stealth wasn't the key, "Nicola?!"

***

Where am I? What...what happened? Oh, God... Ethan!

Nicola's eyes drifted open slowly. Although, she wished she hadn't opened them at all when she looked towards her hands. Ethan was binding them together with duct tape; he'd already dealt with her legs.

"Wait, no, please. What are you doing?" She tried to wriggle free, but he just put more of his weight onto her.

"Just stop Nicola, ok? We both know that you'll come around to my way of thinking eventually. It might take a bit of time, but I'm prepared to wait."

"Where's George...?"

Ethan scoffed and shook his head, "Wow. Even after I bare my soul to you, you still want *him*?" When she didn't respond, he continued, "Well, poor little George should have left us by now. I mean, assuming he's bled out and all."

Nicola didn't focus on the rest of his maniacal speech. All she could think about was George. Was he ok? Where was he? Would anyone find him in time to save him?

She was broken from these thoughts by Ethan clicking his fingers in her face, "Hey, come now. Don't get upset. He was in the way, wasn't he? I needed to take care of him so he wouldn't ruin our time together." He looked her up and down, assessing her body inch by inch, "Speaking of which... where were we?"

He shifted in and out of focus as Nicola tried her best

to stay conscious. Just as her vision was closing in, she heard her voice being called. *I must be dreaming*. She tried to lift her head and then found her voice, "I'm... here..."

Ethan cursed under his breath, "Shit! Oh well... plan B, Sweetness." He smiled at her as he stood up and started scratching and hitting at his own face and neck, clawing and ripping at his clothes. His lip started bleeding and his eye was already beginning to swell as Nicola's vision finally collapsed, "Oh God, Detective? We're over here, we need help. George... George went crazy..."

His voice drifted off into nothingness as she finally gave up her hold on reality.

***

Braum was about to give up the search when he turned the next corner and looked down the corridor. It was crazy to think that he almost didn't look down there. If he hadn't, he wouldn't have seen her. Nicola was lying unconscious on the floor – a small, shallow puddle of blood forming next to her head. He made his way over to her, "Nicola?"

"Oh my God. Thank God you're here. Are you here to help us?"

Braum kept his gun drawn and aimed at Ethan, "Who the hell are you and what are you doing here?"

"Woah I was brought here. Just like Nicola. George brought us both here to kill us. I swear, look at me."

The Detective stared at him, assessing the bruises beginning to form and the blood on his lip. Cautiously, he moved towards them, his gun still aimed, "Are you trying to tell me that George did all of that to you? I just saw him. He has a pretty bad stab wound."

"Yes, well, no... I mean, I did that to him. He was trying to kill us. I wrestled the knife off him and used it. I was defending myself."

Braum narrowed his eyes at Ethan, trying to decide whether or not to believe him. The story made sense, he supposed, but he just couldn't seem to shake the feeling that Ethan was lying to him. His 'Spidey Sense', if you will. "We can go over the story later on when Nicola, Rosemary *and* George wake up."

He noticed the confusion, almost shock, on Ethan's face as he replied, "Wait, they're alive?"

Braum ignored his gut, deciding that Nicola was more important than whatever was wrong with Ethan, "Well give me a hand here. We need to get her downstairs so someone can take a look at her."

15

Once more, the smell of disinfectant stung Nicola's nostrils. Relief momentarily washed over her as she immediately knew where she was. She opened her eyes and scanned her surroundings. Sure enough, she was lying in a hospital bed, the clock ticking on the opposite wall. The only difference this time was that she had a bandage wrapped around her entire head, not just her cheek. Lifting her hand to touch her head, she heard a shuffle and immediately froze. Her stomach dropped as fear gripped her.

"Nicola? It's me." Detective Braum stood from the chair on her left, his hands outstretched in a calming pose, "I know you must be confused but you're safe. You're in the hospital. You've all been here for a couple of days now."

"A couple of days? What happened?"

"What's the last thing that you remember?"

"I don't know... I was... wait, I was upstairs. I was... I was with George and then Ethan... oh my God! Where is he?"

Braum stopped her from getting out of bed, "You can't get up. You've had a serious bump to the head. We're just waiting on the doctor to come and take another look at you."

Nicola resisted but quickly realised that it was an argument she wasn't going to win, "Where is he? Please tell me you got him." Settling back into the bed, she tried to calm her heart rate.

Braum nodded, "We got him. He's quite badly injured in a room down the hall, which he deserves if you ask me."

"He's down the hall? Does he know I'm here? What if he finds me?"

"Nicola, try and relax. You don't have to worry about George anymore. He's handcuffed to the bed and there are guards positioned outside his room."

She wasn't sure if she'd heard him right. Maybe she *was* concussed…their conversation didn't seem to be making any sense, "George is *handcuffed*?"

"You really don't need to worry about him. They're looking after him so well that we'll hopefully be able to formally charge him and eventually send him to trial in no time. As far as I know, he hasn't come around yet, though."

"Why would he need to be arrested and stand trial?" Nicola's pulse kicked up another notch, her brain forming sentences quicker than her mouth could say them. This didn't make sense.

Braum moved closer to the bed as he responded, "Have you heard of Stockholm Syndrome?" When she stared at him blankly he continued, "Stockholm Syndrome is where hostages develop a psychological alliance with their captor as a survival strategy."

Shaking her head, she put her hand up to stop him, "No you don't understand. It wasn't George trying to hurt me. It was Ethan. Ethan attacked us, please, just take me to him. I need to see him."

He shook his head, "It's ok. Stockholm Syndrome is normal and happens a lot in kidnap and abuse situations. There's nothing to be ashamed of."

"You're not listening to me. George. Did. Not. Do. This." Braum ignored her and started moving towards the door, "Wait where are you going? Please just listen to me, Ethan did this, I swear it."

"I'm going to go get someone to check on you. Maybe you need another shot, ok?"

He closed the door and left her alone in the room, sitting in shock. What had Ethan done? Was George stable? Was she going to lose him? Where was Ethan now? She had to know what was going on.

***

Braum discussed Nicola's condition with a passing nurse and asked that she try to calm her down.

Feeling a little confused about Nicola's version of events, he opened the door to Rosemary's room. He peered over his shoulder as he slowly closed the door and saw that she was still asleep. Not surprising given the emergency surgery she'd had to endure. He crept towards the chair at the side of her bed but then noticed that her eyes were open, "I'm sorry, Rosie. I didn't mean to wake you," He whispered.

She managed a slow smile and held her hand out to him. He obliged instantly, quickly closing the distance between them. He took her hand and continued, "How are you feeling now?"

"Like I've just come out of life-saving surgery." She croaked out a laugh, making herself cough.

Braum chuckled and offered her a glass of water, "You scared me for a second there. I thought I'd lost you."

Focusing on his face, she smiled again, "Do you know what I was thinking of as I lay on the ground, hoping I didn't bleed out before I was found?"

He shook his head.

"You, John. You and Stephanie were the only things running through my mind. Everything else seemed to fade away into unimportance. You two were the only constant. I thought for a second that I was going to be with our daughter again, and that brought immense calm and happiness." She reached up to put her hand on his cheek, "Then it hit me that, although I miss her more than anything, it would mean that I would have to leave you. That was a sacrifice I wasn't willing to make."

Braum leaned down and gently kissed her lips. To his excitement and shock, she kissed back. When he broke away, he placed his forehead on hers and smiled as he looked into her eyes, "What does this even mean?"

"Honestly, I don't know. All I know is that I still love you and I hope you still love me too?"

"Rosie, you know I do. How could I not? You're the most amazing woman I've ever met. I was such an idiot to lose you in the first place." They smiled at each other, and he sat down, "I can't believe he almost took you away from me. I told her that George was bad news. Why didn't she listen to me?"

Rosemary winced, trying to sit up further in the bed, "What do you mean? Is George ok?"

Braum rolled his eyes, "Why is everyone so concerned about him? After all he's done."

"I don't understand. George didn't do anything. What do you mean after all he's done?"

"Fine, I'll bite. Like you, he had quite a bad stab wound and is currently handcuffed to his bed a little way down the hall."

"But he didn't do anything. It was Ethan."

His gaze snapped up to hers, "What did you say?"

"It was Ethan. He's the one that killed Nicola's parents, kidnapped her and George and stabbed me. Where is he?"

"Rosie, are you completely sure that it was Ethan?"

"Yes! Why are you quizzing me on this?"

"Ethan says that George is at fault for this. You and Nicola are telling me that it's Ethan?"

Taking a deep breath, she met his gaze, "I swear on everything that I have. Ethan did this."

Braum stood up and paced the room, "I thought there was something strange when I found them. My gut was telling me not to trust him, but I ignored it and helped Nicola." Then it dawned on him, "Oh shit..."

"What? What is it?"

He ran towards the door, ripping it open, "He's in the room next door to Nicola!"

Shouting for officers, he reached Ethan's room and threw the door open. It was too late. Ethan was gone, "Shit!"

The officers drew their weapons, "Sir, what do you need?"

"Comb the hospital and check the CCTV. We need to find the man that was staying in this room." He gave them a description and hurried them away, "I'm going to check on Nicola." He steadied himself and calmly opened the door to her room. The last thing he wanted to do was to scare her; she hadn't even known that Ethan was in the room next door to her. Braum cleared his throat and looked towards the bed. His stomach dropped; she was gone.

***

Nicola opened the bathroom door, her anger at Braum building, "Oh, Detective." When he visibly jumped out of fright, she scoffed, "Come to tell me I'm a liar some more? I can tell you, that's not what I need right now." As she lifted herself back up onto the bed, she could feel the tension radiating from him. He moved towards her and could hardly bring himself to look into her eyes.

"I… Nicola? I've just been speaking with Rosie and she told me that Ethan was the one that hurt both of you, not George." She stared at him in defiance, "I'm so sorry I brushed it off before. I don't want you to worry about that though, because we've doubled up on the guards outside both of your rooms."

Her brows furrowed, "Why?"

"Before we realised Ethan was our perp, he was…" He shook his head before continuing, "…placed in the room next door."

Her pulse quickened and her palms began to sweat as she looked at Braum in disbelief. Trying to get out of bed, she felt the sweat drip down her back.

He put his hands out to stop her, "No please, stay in bed. We need you to stay in this room because..." He cleared his throat, "…well because he's gone."

The words chilled her body. He was free. Free to roam the halls, causing havoc and free to come back for her – which, of course, he would, "He will come back. No amount of protection outside is going to help."

"Nicola, I need you to calm down. There are two police officers outside right now and they have orders to only let me in. Even the doctors and nurses have to be escorted by me. I *will* protect you."

"You can't! He had no trouble with Jones outside my friend's apartment. It wasn't even *my* apartment for God's sake." She broke down, unable to contain it and uncaring of the effect it had on Braum. Eventually wiping her tears and gaining control, she looked back at him, "Do you have any idea where he is... or what he's doing?"

Braum sat in the chair to her right and took a deep breath, "At this moment... honestly, I don't know. We're canvassing the hospital and we will find him. I promise."

Rolling her eyes and nodding, Nicola laughed sarcastically, "Ok, because that went so well the first time.

How's George?"

"He isn't awake yet. The doctors aren't sure when he will be, which is quite normal given the surgery."

"Can I see him?"

"I wouldn't advise it right now. At this point, we need eyes on both of you. It's safer that way for now. I'm sorry."

"I just want to be left alone right now." When he didn't leave, she looked him dead in the eye, "Please just get out. Go and do something useful and find Ethan before he can come back and finish what he started." She couldn't bring herself to look at him as he left the room. In just one conversation, all of the progress she'd made was wiped out. She was back to being the scared little victim that she was at the very beginning of this mess, "Great." She sighed to herself, leaning back onto her pillow.

16

Four days had passed since Braum had dropped the bombshell that Ethan had escaped and, although she shrank back under her covers whenever someone walked past her room, Nicola worried about more than just *her* safety.

While she'd been allowed to see Rosemary, albeit very briefly, she still wasn't allowed to see George. Apparently, he was groggy and had only woken up a handful of times since his emergency surgery. She couldn't stand not knowing what was happening with him. The nurses would only tell her the bare minimum when she asked, "Yes, he's doing fine." "No, he hasn't woken up yet today." "We can't let you see him until he's stable." *Blah blah blah.*

Sighing, she picked up the remote for the television and tried to distract herself from her thoughts, finally settling on some show about home renovations. It was the best of a bad bunch, really.

A few hours had gone by when there was a knock at her door. She jumped slightly and dropped the remote. Holding her breath, she waited for someone to speak from the other side.

"Excuse me? Ma'am?" The door opened and a police officer stood in the doorway.

His face was familiar to her; he was one of the few that she trusted. *Richard*s. Braum had introduced her to only a handful of police officers that he trusted to guard her room. She was just thankful that she didn't have to deal with Braum all the time, "I just wanted to let you know that we're switching guard cover for the evening. Veers and Jordan are going to be outside your room all night." He opened the door further so that she could see them. Another two that she had seen but not spoken to, "And if you need anything, just let them know."

Looking past his shoulder to the officers on the plastic seats, she spoke plainly, "Are they as good as you, Richards?"

He smiled, "Of course. Detective Braum handpicked all of us because he knows we're the best for the job. Really, you have nothing to worry about. Everything is in—"

He was cut off by shouting down the hall. Grabbing a nurse that was hurrying past, he asked what was going on. "Room 221. Something's happened to his machines." The nurse said, barely stopping to speak.

"221? That's George's room." Nicola thrashed at her covers, trying to get out of bed.

Richards put his hand out to her as he backed out of the room, "No! You stay where you are and do not move." Richards and Jordan took off running down the hall. Richards called back over his shoulder for Veers to stay in Nicola's room and keep the door shut.

As much as she hated not being able to help, she took the order and stayed in bed. She stopped fidgeting when Veers closed the door. He stood next to it, his hand unbuttoning his holster. He turned and caught her looking at his hand. Her cheeks warmed but he smiled reassuringly at her, "It's just a precaution. No need to worry."

After a few minutes, there was a knock and a voice spoke through the door, "It's Officer Durand, sir. Detective Braum sent me to relieve you. He needs you down there." With some trepidation, Veers opened the door. He checked out the badge and uniform of the officer and must have been happy with what he saw, because he opened the door further and turned to Nicola, "Stay here, Miss Evans. We will be back with an update soon." She nodded at him; her knees pulled up to her chest.

Nicola registered the blue of the officer's uniform and the badge on his chest. She couldn't see his face thanks to the low power of the lights but spoke anyway, "Hey, hi?" When his head slightly turned towards her, she carried on, "Do you know what's happening in room 221? Is George ok?"

"Ma'am, I don't know. I was just told to come in here and stay with you."

Nicola knew that voice. It seemed slightly distorted, but she knew it. The officer still hadn't turned towards her, his stance tough and ready, "Oh, well… I'm sorry. Have we met? I'm sure I recognise your voice…"

Ignoring her he walked for the door, pulling a key from his pocket, and locked it from the inside. There was a *clink!* and Nicola realised he'd snapped the key off in the lock. She slid herself backwards up the bed and tried to steady her breathing. *The alarm*, her brain screamed out. Nicola glanced around for it, trying not to make any sound. Her heart sank when she noticed that it was set on the table at the foot of the bed.

"Oh, I wouldn't worry about the alarm by the way. I think they're a bit too busy to deal with you at the moment."

Nicola's heart stopped and her blood ran cold, "Ethan."

He turned to her, that familiar grin spread across his face.

***

"What happened in here?" Braum burst through the door to room 221, sweat beading on his face. His question was met by silence.

He was about to speak louder when a nurse grabbed his arm, "I'm sorry sir, but you can't be in here. You'll all have to leave right now."

"Hey!" He shouted, "I am Detective Braum. I'm the lead in this investigation, and you will tell me right now what has happened in here." The nurse visibly gulped and he felt terrible, but needed answers. She ushered him into the corridor to give the nurses some privacy to work.

Clearing her throat, she said, "Well, Detective... An alarm was tripped in room 221. When we got in there, we saw that this young man's I.V.s were ripped out and thrown on the floor." She motioned towards the floor, "As well as that, the cables controlling this young man's heart monitor were detached. Now, they don't just make a habit of falling out on their own, if you get my meaning?"

"Wait...are you saying that someone did this?"

Richards spoke, "I'm here, sir. What do you need?"

"What are you doing here? You're supposed to be down the hall with Miss Evans?"

"Yes, sir, but Officer Durand said that you needed me

here."

"Durand? Who the hell is Officer Du—" It was as if a light bulb had gone off in his head. He couldn't believe he hadn't seen it before, "He's here!" He shouted as he ran from the room.

"Excuse me? Who's here?"

"Ethan! George is a distraction!"

The officers followed him out of the room and down to Nicola's, "Why the hell is the door shut?"

"Sir, the door's locked. We can't get in!"

"Well bust it down!"

"We tried! It's like the door is reinforced, or someone has broken a key off in the lock."

"Use a Goddamn fire extinguisher or get the maintenance man!" Braum turned to grab the nurse, "Where is the key to this room?"

She shook her head, "It should be up at the nurse's station. I'll have to go get it."

"Go! Now!"

When the nurse was out of sight, Braum banged on the door, "Nicola? Can you hear me?" When he was met with silence, he couldn't help but wonder if he might be too late.

***

"Ethan? Please... what have you done to George?"

He set his hat down on the chair as he responded, "No, no I don't want to talk about him. I'm done talking about him. With any luck he'll be dead by now anyway."

A tear hit her cheek before she even knew that she was crying.

He spoke again, "Oh, you don't know how difficult it's been these past few days. Having to wait for the perfect moment to execute my plan. It's been torture, Nicola."

She stared at him, swallowing down her own vomit. *Pull yourself together*, she thought. *Keeping him calm is the only way you're going to make it through this.* "You're right, Ethan. I'm sorry. I won't mention him again, I swear."

Ethan's head snapped sideways as someone - Braum, Nicola presumed - pounded on the door.

"Nicola? Can you hear me?"

Ethan rushed to her bedside, reaching out his hand to cover her mouth. "Oh no. No, you're not going to speak to him either."

She stiffened at his touch, nodding.

"Ok... now it's going to take them a while to get in here. I've given them the run-around, you see. They need a specific key to get in here and, I think it may have gone missing...it probably doesn't help that I've blocked the lock, too!" That horrible grin spread across his face as he stared at her, lowering his hand. He walked back over to the door, laughing and mocking Braum as he went.

Taking a deep breath, while Ethan was entranced by his own monologue, she pulled back the covers. Nicola kept her eyes focused on him as she carefully placed her feet on the floor. She stood and began slowly making her way over to the table; aiming for the cutlery set that had been placed there the previous mealtime. A fork... and a knife. Fighting against her better judgement, she moved her gaze over to the table as she got closer. Unfortunately for her, she hadn't seen the cup on the floor. She felt the impact of her foot hitting the cup before the sound registered. Her heart stopped and she froze.

There was a split second of complete silence and then Ethan broke through it in a rage. He flew at her and pinned her against the wall, "Why won't you just admit it? Why won't you believe that we're meant to be together? Why else would fate bring you back to me? In the apartment that night, that wasn't a coincidence."

"No, we're not! You are a psychopath! Why are you so fixated on me?!"

He moved closer to her, snarling in her face like a wild animal, "Don't... call... me... that..."

"That's exactly what you are. You're damaged!"

His composure broke. Ethan threw Nicola to the floor and started pacing, "I don't *want* to hurt you, you know. You just, you just keep pushing me. Why do you keep pushing me? It's like you want me to hurt you."

She pulled herself across the floor and away from him, unable to stand.

"Oh now, where are you going? I've told you..."

Ethan stalked across the room and bent down over her, "They're not getting in here that way and you aren't getting out that way."

"Why are you doing this? Think about it – if *I* can't get out, then *you* can't get out!"

"Oh… Nicola, come on. I'll take all of them down and easily get out of here with you. We either both make it out of here, or none of us will."

"Please, Ethan...please can we just stop this now? Why won't you leave me alone? This is insane."

Ethan smiled down at her and lowered himself towards her, his knees on either side of her. She tried to slide out of his reach, but he reached around behind her and pulled her closer to him.

"Ethan, wait... wait, please..."

"Wait for what? Hm? Wait so that they have time to break through that door? Wait so that they have time to save you? Is that what you want?" He leaned closer and stared straight at her. Nicola knew at that moment. She knew that it didn't matter how long it took Braum and the other officers to get into the room. Ethan was going to do whatever he wanted, however he wanted, and she probably wasn't going to leave the room alive.

She retreated into herself and tried to believe that she was somewhere else. *I hope George is ok. I hope they got to him in time to help him. I hope Rosemary is doing ok. Braum will need her when this all goes south.*

She didn't even register the sound of the door slamming against the wall as Braum broke through it.

***

A troop of officers piled into the room behind him, guns drawn and awaiting orders.

The room was a mess. The bed was disheveled and there was food everywhere - from the previous meal, he assumed. Off to the side, Braum noticed movement. Ethan was perched over Nicola on the floor, his hands on either side of her, holding himself steady with his face buried in her hair. Nicola looked like she'd completely given up. Corpse-like, almost. Her face was blank, and her stare was vacant; she was focused on the clock on the opposite wall.

"Hey! Get the hell off her." He raised his gun and aimed straight at Ethan.

Ethan was smarter than Braum gave him credit for, standing and holding her in front of him. He knew that Braum would never shoot her. That's when she snapped out of the spell that she'd been under and started struggling.

"Stay still!" Ethan growled.

"Come on, Ethan. Don't do this. You can still walk out of here." Braum wanted to keep Ethan's attention for as long as possible. That was the only way to protect Nicola.

"You're even dumber than I thought. Of course we're walking out of here, and you're going to let us go."

Braum held his ground, keeping his gun trained on Ethan. Waiting for the perfect shot, "I can't let you do that, son. You can still walk out of here with me, but Nicola stays."

"See, that's where you've got it wrong." Ethan tightened his grip on Nicola, pulling the knife from his pocket. He raised it to her throat and stared at Braum, "We're leaving right now, and you're not going to try and stop us." He started slowly moving forwards, never once taking his eyes off of Braum.

"Don't move." Braum barked.

Ethan smiled, "Ok... ok, Mr. Tough Guy. Take your shot. If you're sure that you can take me down before I slide this blade across her throat."

Braum couldn't risk it. As much as he hated it, he knew that Ethan was right. If he took a shot now, Nicola was definitely dead. He had to get Ethan to move the knife away from her throat. If he did that, Braum knew he could take him. "Why are you doing this, Ethan? Were you hurt as a child or are you just a plain, good old-fashioned psycho?"

Ethan laughed, "A psycho? No, no, no. I'm much more than that. I'm..." He chuckled, "... I'm a genius."

"Really? How you figure that?"

"You know the rape charge that you found in George's file? Me. I did that to precious George. No one figured it out, not even the police. So, you tell me, how is that *not* genius?"

Braum took his chance, "Well, I guess I just have a hard time believing that you're a genius, instead of an impotent, self-centered psychopath who has to hurt and kill people to get off."

"Shut up."

He had him. He had to keep pushing his buttons. If he could rattle him, maybe he would move the knife…just enough. "Hey fellas, can you give Ethan and me a minute?" Braum ushered the officers out of the room without taking his eyes off Ethan, "Oh sorry. Did I hit a sore spot?"

"What are you doing?" Nicola coughed out, staring at Braum with wide eyes.

"Yes, Detective. What *are* you doing?"

"Me? I'm just trying to get to know you, Ethan. Find out what makes you tick. So, was it mummy that hurt you when you were little? Or no, was it daddy?"

Ethan stared at Braum through narrowed eyes, "I'm warning you."

"Come on then, Ethan. Come and show me what you can do to someone in a fair fight."

***

It was at that moment that Nicola made a decision – probably the most important of her life. She was through being a victim. Tired of having someone else control her life, her movements – even her emotions. She glanced up at Braum, his gun drawn and aimed, using her eyes to tell him what she was going to do. The realisation flashed across his face mere seconds before she acted. Summoning all of her strength, she reached up and dug her nails into Ethan's forearm, pulling his arm away from her.

Precious centimeters – that was all she needed to get the knife away from her throat.

A shot rang out.

17

Nicola shook from side to side, a motion that pulled her back to reality, and slowly opened her eyes.

"Nicola? Nicola, can you hear me?"

There was a weight on top of her, and a sharp pain in her head, although she didn't understand why. She looked down, finding Ethan's lifeless eyes staring up at her, "Get him off me," she screamed, flailing as she tried to push him away. It didn't work – he was too heavy, so she tried the only thing she could think of. Nicola balled her fist and began hitting him, in the hopes that it would keep him from harming her.

She heard Braum call her name but couldn't stop herself. Not until he grabbed her arm mid-hit. That's when she noticed the blood trickling from her hand and dripping silently to the floor. She looked down, shocked to see that her hospital gown had been stained crimson. The blood couldn't have all been hers. Nicola glanced back to Ethan and noticed that his head had fallen to the side, revealing a large, gaping wound with jagged edges where his ear once sat.

She immediately began hyperventilating.

Braum instructed another officer to lift Ethan, as he hooked his arms around Nicola and lifted her backwards, "It's ok, I've got you. You're safe now."

"Why...what is...what happ—"

Braum had to stop her from turning and looking at Ethan's body, "Don't look over there, Nicola. You don't need to look at him anymore." He supported her arm, "Oh no...don't move too quickly. You've had a nasty bump on the head, so we need to get you checked out again."

She lifted a hand to her head and panic set in once again when she saw her own blood spilling down her left arm.

"Hold this to your head and apply pressure. Nicola?" Braum caught her attention by waving a hand in front of her, "Nicola? Make sure you apply pressure, or it'll just keep bleeding."

She looked down, trying to focus on something as

small as moving her feet.

Braum led her to a chair in the corridor and sat her down. He looked at her, shaking his head as he spoke.

Nicola didn't register what he was saying. She just stared down at her clothes and completely zoned out. The blood was all over her, "Oh my God... I don't... I can't breathe!" She shook her head, trying to get her breathing under control but failing completely.

Braum spoke softly and held her arm, "Here, Nicola. Let's go into the other room, ok? You're fine. I've got you." He ushered her into a separate room and closed the door behind them.

As soon as the door was shut Nicola screamed, falling to the floor. Without thinking, Braum dropped to the floor and held her, letting her cry and hit when she needed, "Shh, you're ok. Everything is ok now. He's gone, Nicola, I promise."

"But I just... I don't understand..." She managed to squeak through sobs, "There's so much blood!"

Braum shook his head as he cradled her to his chest, "I had a clear shot and I took it. I couldn't risk him hurting you."

She struggled to think straight.

"I'm sorry you had to see that," Braum said, "Tell you what – I'll get one of the nurses to clean up your head and take you to a shower room? You can wash and change. You might feel a bit better."

Nicola nodded, "I want to see George after."

Braum agreed as he led her from the room.

***

As Nicola stood under the running water, she tried to make sense of what'd happened in that hospital room. She wasn't stupid, nor was she naïve. She knew that Ethan was dead and finally out of her life, but she just couldn't make sense of it.

A quick knock on the door scared Nicola half to death. She shut off the water, pulled a towel around herself and then unlocked the door.

"Hello, Nicola?" It was a nurse she hadn't seen before, "I thought you'd want to know that George is awake and asking for you again."

Nicola smiled at the mention of George's name. A smile that quickly faded when the extractor fan kicked in and she almost dropped the towel. Ethan was gone but every noise still elicited fear.

"I'm so sick of this already." She bit out through gritted teeth, letting her frustration show.

She'd actually been allowed to sit with George a few times, but he had always been asleep. The nurses said he was more comfortable that way. Today, though, he might be awake and know she was there.

She opened the door to his room and was greeted by that same warm smile that she saw the very first time they met.

"Hey, stranger. What's happening?"

"Hi, how are you feeling?"

George smiled, motioning to the chair next to him, "I'm feeling a lot better now that I've had some decent sleep. Probably the one thing I can thank my mini-coma for."

Nicola got herself comfy in the chair and painted on a smile, "That's amazing. I'm so happy you're doing better. Have the nurses said when you'll be ready to discharge?"

He shook his head, "No they haven't said yet. Apparently, I'm still considered critical, so they need to keep me in a little while longer."

"Ah, that's… well, at least they're keeping an eye – " She'd held it back for as long as she could, but Nicola just couldn't keep it together. She started bawling.

George panicked and held her hand, "Hey, hey it's not that bad. I'm sure I'll be fine! What's wrong?"

Trying to slow her breathing, Nicola shook her head, "No, it's not that… it's just… Ethan."

At the sound of his name George stiffened, holding Nicola's hand tight – almost *too* tight, "What has that son of a bitch done now? Didn't they catch him?"

She took a deep breath, choosing her words carefully before she said them, "Well, when they found us upstairs, only Ethan was conscious. Braum didn't have anything to go on

97

other than his word."

He looked at her, the confusion showing on his face, "Wait, what? I don't understand…"

"Well because you and I were out cold when they found us, Ethan told them that you were the one that hurt me and that he had to put you down to save me."

"But… how could they believe that?"

"That's the only version of the story they had. Until I woke up and told them different – oh, and Rosemary as well. Braum finally listened to us and doubled-up on security. He'd had the bright idea of putting Ethan in the room next door to me because he was *such a good guy*."

George began ripping the tubes out of his arms, a troop of machines beeping in unison, "Where is he?"

Nicola put a hand on his shoulder as she tried to hold him in place, "No, no you don't understand… he's not here."

"They let him get away?"

"Not exactly."

He waved his hand at her in confusion, "Wait, what do you mean?"

She took a deep breath as she began explaining the eventful evening to him, watching as his face shifted from worried, to upset to flat-out furious.

"Oh my God, are you ok? How are you sitting here right now? I mean, how are you not freaking out?"

Nicola looked straight at George, "Of course I'm freaking out. Every noise? I'm convinced he's back. Every shadow? I convince myself that it's him. I had a nap while I was waiting to use the shower room – I wasn't asleep for more than a few minutes before his face popped into my mind." She had to stop talking. She didn't want to ramble George back into a coma.

Her speech had quite the opposite effect though; it made him even more furious that she was put in that position.

***

It took a few hours, but Nicola was finally able to calm George down.

"Now you need to keep yourself calm and leave these

in your arm, George. Come on. You know these are for your benefit!" The nurse scolded him as she turned to leave the room.

Once she'd closed the door, Nicola shook her head and let out a sigh, "Look, what does it matter? He's out of our lives now, and we'll be out of here soon. We can get everything back to normal... if you want that?"

"What do you mean *if*?"

She cleared her throat, "Well, I didn't exactly treat you very well the last time we spoke, did I? That just goes to show how stupid I can be, I guess."

George nodded, "M-hm, that's true. I mean... you did slap me..."

Nicola dropped her head, her cheeks flushing with embarrassment. *Why am I such an idiot?*

"It's ok, I understand. If I was you, I wouldn't want to be around me either. I just wanted to come by and make sure you were ok..." She stood up, backing towards the door, "...and to thank you for everything you've done for me. You saved my life and I won't ever be able to repay that." Just before she reached the door, she took one last look at George – that perfect, lovely, trusting face – and turned away. As she placed her hand on the doorknob, he called out to her from the bed.

"Hey! Where are you going? Get back over here, you silly sod."

She couldn't help the smile that spread across her face as she made her way back over to the chair. She wasn't ok but she was ready. Ready for the future. Ready for her recovery process.

18

Nicola looked around the garden, taking time to register each person – Rosemary, Braum and, perhaps the most important to her, George.

She couldn't believe that they were all there; the only people that knew how she felt. They were bonded together in a way no one would ever understand. It was a miracle that they were all in one spot enjoying a barbeque and some drinks, with the sun beating down. *Mum would have loved the sun today and Dad…oh, he would have loved the burgers.* She thought to herself as she watched the birds; the breeze lightly ruffling the trees. *Most of all, they would have both loved George.*

Six months had passed since the shooting at the hospital, and Nicola's nightmares were finally starting to subside with the help of regular therapy and the patience of George.

She still had trouble with loud noises, and dimly lit - or dark - areas but she was trying to fight through it by using headphones around constructions sites and always keeping a torch in her bedside drawer. She wanted to get stronger and wanted her friends to be proud of her. She craved the simple, everyday things that meant that things were getting back to normal.

"Earth to Nicola!" Rosemary laughed as she sat down next to her, watching the men cook.

"What?"

"You looked completely zoned out then. Are you ok?"

Nicola laughed, "Yeah, I'm fine. I was just thinking about everything. Mum and dad would've loved you guys."

Rosemary smiled and put a reassuring hand and Nicola's arm, "I'm so sorry that they're not here to see how everything has panned out. They'd have been so proud of how strong you are, and how far you've come."

Both women shared a gaze and tears were quickly replaced by laughs when they heard the string of cussing and frustration coming from their partners.

"Men – can't live with them, can't kill them!"

"I suppose that's why we love them, though. What would we do without them?"

Rosemary leaned closer, "Well we wouldn't have any entertainment now, would we?"

"Hey, babe?" Nicola called out, "Do you need some help? We don't mind coming over if you do?"

She was cut off almost instantly, George trying to sound polite, "No, no. You stay there. We've got this under control."

"Ok, I love you!"

"Love you, too…"

His voice trailed off and the women started giggling again. Nicola took a sip of her Margarita and coughed, "Wow… did you make these Rosemary?"

"Of course. You didn't want a boring drink, did you?"

"So, how are you and Braum doing? I'm sorry – John?"

A smile spread across Rosemary's face, and the warmth that radiated from her was just beautiful to see, "We're really good. He took such great care of me that I never wanted for anything after leaving the hospital. It's quite bittersweet really. We're learning how to be together again and how to help each other live with the loss of our sweet Stephanie."

"For what it's worth," Now it was Nicola's turn to hold Rosemary's hand, "You both seem happy together and I'm so happy that fate brought you back together." In an attempt to lighten the mood, she continued, "And I never knew that John was capable of smiling!"

They laughed, less than flattering snorts emerging but they didn't care.

A faint ringing caught Nicola's ear, but Braum was way ahead of her, with his keen Detective hearing, "Is that the phone?"

"Yeah, it is. I'll get it." Nicola responded.

"Thanks, babe." George called back.

Sure, it was his holiday home, but she practically lived there now so he had no problem with her answering the phone.

She skipped into the house, still laughing from her chat with Rosemary. Smiling, she picked up the phone, "Yello?" There was slight static, so she asked again, "Sorry, the line's breaking up. Hello?"

Silence…she was about to hang up when she thought she heard something.

It couldn't be…

Low, heavy breathing…

THE END

Printed in Great Britain
by Amazon

64529107R00064